Forsaking All Others

BY

SHANNON MYERS

To Ellen -
enjoy!

Cover Design by: The Final Wrap

Photographers: DesLaurier Media/Sheridan Davis

Models: Travis DesLaurier & Ashley Williams

Formatting & Interior Design: Daryl Banner

First Printing: 2016

ISBN 978-0-9975348-4-9

DISCLAIMER: This story contains disturbing situations, graphic violence, sex, and strong language. This could be a trigger for some. That being said, it does have a happily ever after.

DEDICATION

This book is dedicated to my readers.

Thank you for loving David & Elizabeth

as much as I do and for taking a chance

on a new author.

Acknowledgements

This book wouldn't have been possible without some pretty amazing people.

Zach – Thank you for supporting this crazy dream of mine. You're always up for being my soundboard, even though it ruins the surprise for you. Z+S. Always, my love.

Parker & Owen – You're both so proud of Mama's story, even though you'll never be allowed to read it. Thank you for telling everyone we meet about it. I love you both to the moon and back.

Jennifer & Olivia – Thank you for being my Lauren. Every good writer needs a redheaded best friend. I'm lucky enough to have two. You're both the best unpaid PAs I could ever want. I see many patio nights in our future.

Sheridan – Thank you for taking such beautiful pictures. You captured exactly what I wanted. You're the best awkward penguin I know.

Rebecca – God bless you. Thank you for having the patience of a saint when it comes to me and my book covers. I know you secretly enjoy my last minute changes. If I ever make it to Arizona, I am bringing you a big bottle of wine and we'll have porch karaoke.

Ashley – Thank you for being my own personal hair savior and an absolutely stunning cover model. You made the perfect Elizabeth and maybe someday, we can get you and Travis together for pictures.

Travis – Thank you for agreeing to work with me and for providing the perfect picture to use for the cover. You took David's character seriously and I will forever be grateful.

To my readers – This book wouldn't have been possible without the support I received from all of you. Every review and rating pushed me to make this story perfect. All of the feedback went toward giving you all the happy ending you deserve.

I wanted my book to be as factually accurate as possible and these amazing people helped me do just that.

Celeste Botros – Thank you for your expert advice in family law. While it didn't play out like a courtroom drama, your advice ensured that the story remained realistic.

Christi Wilson – I'm so glad you enjoyed the first book. Thank you for taking time out of your day to answer my labor and delivery questions. Your input was crucial to the story.

Lindsey Pierson – Thank you for sharing your birth story with me. Hays is truly a miracle and I'm glad that we get to see him at the office.

Elizabeth Addington – Thank you for patiently answering all of my questions regarding medevac transport. Writing a scene like that seemed daunting until I talked with you. Your expertise lent a lot of credibility to David and Elizabeth's story.

TABLE OF CONTENTS

PROLOGUE

Beth

Once upon a time there was a beautiful princess. She didn't see the world as everyone else did and that made her anxious. She thought she was destined to live a life of solitude locked inside the castle of her emotions until she met him. The dashing prince literally swept her off of her feet inside an enchanted bar one evening and she swore she'd never feel with anyone what she felt with him. The dashing young prince asked the beautiful princess to marry him and she agreed. They lived happily ever after...for a while.

The King died unexpectedly, leaving the prince to manage the entire kingdom alone. He was distraught and nothing the princess did could shake him from his grief. Even worse, there was an evil enchantress, masquerading as the princess's best friend. She waited patiently before casting a spell over the prince and claiming him as her own.

Another prince arrived from a foreign land. The princess fell hard and began spending all of her time with him. The prince and princess took their fairy tale and fucked it up beyond repair while their kingdom burned down around them.

FORSAKING ALL OTHERS

CHAPTER
ONE
David

My Dad was the best man I'd ever known. He worked his ass off making a life for me and my mom. He'd be at work before the sun was fully out most days and he wouldn't pull into the driveway until it set. He ran his own construction company and I wanted nothing more than to follow in his footsteps.

My mom said I was always tagging along, eager to be near him—needing to just be in his presence. I could call him up, no matter the problem, and he'd always be willing to offer advice. He was just that kind of person. The man stood over six feet tall and had his arms sleeved in tattoos. He even drove a Harley, just to complete his bad ass biker look. He looked a little rough around the edges, but I watched how he was with Mom. That man would've given his life for her at any moment. It was like she was the fucking sun and he was content to spend his days revolving around her.

There were countless times that I'd walk into the kitchen or living room only to find the two of them making out like a couple of teenagers. At the time, I didn't pay much attention to it—I thought everyone's parents were like that. It wasn't until I was much older that I realized how rare of a thing it was—this passion they still had for each other, even decades later.

I assumed I'd marry and my marriage would be just like theirs. Hell, I grew up surrounded by this love they shared, how could it not? I dated some, but with the bar set so high, I knew it was going to take someone special to catch my eye.

That night at *Nick's*, I was beyond exhausted and had tried to get out of going out, but Mike was having none of that. I was just about to call it a night when the most beautiful woman I'd ever seen in my life fell into my arms, dousing me in pineapple and rum.

Beth was this teeny-tiny little thing with a fetish for large heels that were damn near impossible for her to walk in. She was incredibly funny and sarcastic as hell—and I knew she was the one within five minutes of talking to her. She was clumsy and had a tendency to say whatever was in her head without considering the consequences. And I wanted nothing more than to be her man, to wake up next to that mess of blonde curls for the rest of my life.

The first time I took her down to my parent's house, my dad pulled me aside. He said he'd seen the look on my face one other time; when he was looking in a mirror thirty-five years ago. We were sitting on their back porch drinking beer when he spoke up.

"David, Elizabeth is something special. You love her?"

I grinned at him, "Yeah, I damn sure do."

He tipped his beer in my direction, "Well, then don't waste any more time and get a goddamn ring on that girl's hand before someone else does!"

So, I listened to my old man and I proposed. We were happy, until the business took center stage and I stopped noticing the way her nose crinkled when she was trying not to laugh or how her hair looked almost golden in direct sunlight. I didn't notice anything unless it was construction related.

One evening my dad called me up to talk about it. I tried making excuses, but he was having none of it.

"David, I watched her when we were there a week ago. She's

not okay with you being gone this much. A marriage can't work like that."

"Dad, I know, I just need to get this off the ground and I don't know—we'll take a trip. Get back to normal."

"Son, I don't think you need to wait. The business can wait, but I saw the look in her eyes—this resignation. You can't put this on the back burner right now."

"Fuck, Dad, I'm under a lot of pressure here." I added sarcastically, "We can't all run a business like you." It was a low blow, but I wanted him to see all the labor going into Greene Construction, not get tied up with thoughts of my marriage failing.

"I love you and her both, David. I just don't want to see you two grow apart. You've got something special. Don't take it for granted."

I didn't answer him right away.

"David—"

"Yeah, Dad, I've got another call coming in. I'll talk to you later." I ended the call.

The next morning Beth and I sat on the patio together—the first weekend that we'd had to ourselves in a long time. I was watching her drink her coffee and I thought that maybe my dad was right when my phone rang.

"Hey Mom."

"David—" Her voice broke and I knew something was wrong, "Your dad…he…he had a heart attack. Sweetie, he's gone."

I hung up after failing miserably at trying to comfort her. Everything felt surreal. My dad—gone. The biker who never got so much as a cold—dead.

I told Beth and she immediately began sobbing and asking me questions. I got up and walked away from her—needing to be alone. It wasn't until I was under the shower head, scalding water hitting my body that I realized I never told him I loved him back. My old man wanted nothing more than to see me happy and I didn't even tell him I loved him during our last conversation.

CHAPTER
TWO
David

It's been six weeks. Six hellish weeks without her. I've been living in hotel rooms and while I originally tried to make sure all my jobs were done close to home, I've had to take some out of town jobs in order to ensure all of our bills remain paid while Beth's recuperating. I've also tried to stop by and see her a few times, but each time I show up, I'm met with the door in my face.

While I've been actively trying to put my marriage back together, I've been dodging calls and texts from Jess. When I told her that Beth knew everything, I expected her to show some remorse. I couldn't have been more wrong. She seemed happy by the news and almost immediately began trying to plan our future together. It's like she couldn't get it through her thick skull that I wasn't going to throw away my marriage and my life over several instances of drunken, meaningless sex. Unfortunately, Jess doesn't give up that easily. Between that and her pregnancy, I'm screwed.

I rub at my eyes as the phone rings. I haven't slept in days. As I lift my arm, I smell myself. *"David, you really need to shower."* The memory of her whispering in my ear as she lay in that hospital bed after the wreck is almost enough to overtake me. Mike finally picks up, saving me from my emotions.

"Detective Sullivan speaking."

"Don't you just sound real professional, Detective," I put on a thick southern drawl in an attempt to throw him off.

"Nice try, dickwad. You still drowning your worries in a bottle of Pendleton?"

I sigh, "No, I gave that shit up. I'm not going to get her back drinking like that."

I can hear him clicking a pen on and off, it's a nervous habit he's had as long as I can remember.

"So, she's still shutting you out? What did I tell you that night you both got home from the hospital? I told you the lies were going to come back and bite you in the ass, didn't I?"

His words leave a sour taste in my mouth, "Yeah, you did. I just thought we were getting a second chance—a clean slate. You ever find out anything on Landon?"

Mike clears his throat, "He's clean, David. Guy doesn't even have so much as a speeding ticket. So, there's no chance of me bringing him in and holding him indefinitely as you so helpfully recommended the other night. Why are you so focused on him?"

"I don't know, Mike. I just have a bad feeling about this guy. The way he looked at her, acting as though she was his possession—I still think he's the one who broke into the house that night—"

He cuts me off, "David, we've been over this. No prints were ever recovered and when we questioned him, he had a rock solid alibi. He's not the perp. Tell you what, I know you haven't had a decent meal in quite a while. I'm taking off around five tonight, let's meet for dinner."

"Where?" The idea of eating a meal at a table and not in my truck is really appealing right now.

FORSAKING ALL OTHERS

"I'd say *Nick's*, but I don't wanna send you on a bender again. Let's just meet at West End and grab some pizza."

I agree and forty-five minutes later, after a long shower and a change of clothes, I'm sitting across from him. I'm messing around with the coaster my beer is resting on when he interrupts.

"So—she won't see you, but is she still seeing him?"

I stiffen immediately and my jaw clenches, "I don't know—I guess I just assumed she was keeping us both at a distance while she sorted everything out."

He takes a swig from his bottle of Guinness and nods, "I know I asked when you first told me, but did you ever suspect she was screwing someone else?"

I struggle to find the right words as I mull it over. Beth was always so happy to have me home, she'd practically throw herself at me the minute I'd come through the door. *Maybe out of guilt?* It's as if a bucket of ice water has been thrown on me and I feel physically sick from it.

It was right in front of my face the whole time—the house was always spotless, and I knew for a fact she cleaned like that to deal with stress. That, and she startled at the slightest sound. It's how I'd gotten away with my crimes against her, we were both so preoccupied with our own guilt that we missed each other's.

I finally find my voice again, "I never saw anything out of the ordinary. Looking back on it though, the signs were there."

We've fallen back into a comfortable silence when a beautiful woman with long blonde hair walks up. She looks so much like Beth, I have to do a double take.

She smiles uncertainly, "David Greene?"

I nod, encouraging her to continue.

She thrusts a large manila envelope in my hands and looks

almost apologetic as she does so.

"You've been served."

CHAPTER THREE
Beth

Cheater. Adulteress. Unfaithful. Philanderer. Fraud. The words are on a constant replay in my mind. I'm still struggling to make sense of all of my memories—to sort fact from fiction. What I do remember is enough to disgust me. I alternate daily on whether I hate David or myself more.

I feel like a part of me knew about what went on with David and "she who shall not be named," enough for my brain to leave me bread crumbs at least. And can we pause for a moment to think about the level of assholery one must be at to call up their best friend to come take care of them when they're actively screwing said friend's husband and their own spouse has left?

"Right after my Dad died—and then the night you admitted you were on birth control. I took off and ended up drunk in a bar. She showed up and uh, one thing led to another." My throat burns at the memory of his confession and in remembering that it was Jess who suggested that I get on birth control in the first place. The bitch suggested it and then used it against me to get my husband into her bed. My best friend.

I waited six weeks, hoping there'd be some clear answer on how to fix everything. There wasn't. He and I were two people who had hurt each other beyond reconciliation. I did the only thing I knew to do. I finally Googled "How to file for divorce in Texas," and they were going to be serving him the papers within the next few days.

I couldn't face him on my own and I knew there was no way in hell he'd agree to it. If I had to talk to him face to face about my decision, he'd either end up in bed with me or on the floor bleeding out. *Yeah, the man stirs up some pretty conflicting feelings within me.* No, it was safer this way. Plus, with Jess having his baby— ugh, I may vomit—I had no other choice. I wasn't willing to stay with him, somehow try to get past all the hurt we'd caused each other, all while playing step-mom to Jess's kid. That was daytime talk show-level crazy.

"You still think this is the best idea?" Lauren walks into the living room with a large cardboard box. She places it on the coffee table and searches for a marker to label it.

I take my glasses off and rub my eyes. God, I'm exhausted. I'm not sure if it's due to the accident or if all of the emotional bullshit is finally taking its toll.

"Laur—I can't stay. He's going to want the house for his... his—" I place a hand over my mouth as I begin dry heaving. *Yeah, I'm not ever going to feel comfortable discussing my husband and my former best friend having a baby together.* I make my way into the kitchen and vomit into the sink, as it's the closest thing to me.

"Damn, Elizabeth. Have you gone a day in the past few weeks without vomiting when someone brings up David?"

I rinse the sink and my mouth out with water while giving a weak shrug. I can feel the tears forming, right on cue, because it's not enough to be sick—I have to become an emotional basket case as well. I can't stop crying lately. If I didn't know better I'd think I was—*oh sweet Jesus.*

"Lauren, we need to run to the pharmacy."

FORSAKING ALL OTHERS

Two minutes. The longest two minutes of my life. I sit on the edge of the bathtub, my legs bouncing and my head in my hands while Lauren paces.

"How did this happen?"

I pop my head up long enough to give her a look, "Really?"

"Stop, we don't need it."

He looks over his shoulder at me, "Are you sure? We don't have to try tonight."

"I want to do this and I really want to feel you inside of me. Nothing else...please."

Those words are coming back to bite me now, aren't they? I cannot be pregnant. Not right now. Six weeks ago? Sure. I thought my life was a fairy tale.

My phone chimes at me, letting me know it's been two minutes. Lauren stops pacing and we just stare uncertainly at each other.

"You want me to look?"

I nod and she grabs the test off the back of the toilet. When she bites her lip, I know.

"It's positive, love. You're pregnant."

"Okay. Okay. Don't panic. It's probably wrong. The test is wrong. We just need to go out and um, buy a different brand." I can hear the hysteria in my voice.

She sits down on the rug near my feet. "Let's call David. He has a right to know."

I rub my eyes, "No. I cannot do that to him. Make him choose between me and...her." I say the word "her" with as much disgust as I can muster.

"I've said it before and I'll say it again: If Jess is really pregnant, then I'm the Queen of England. Call him."

I place my hand on her shoulder, "No. No one can know about this. I just need a minute to think."

CHAPTER FOUR

David

"You've been served." I thought up until this point the worst three words I'd ever heard were, "David, I'm pregnant," but this was worse. Far worse. To say I was blindsided by it would be the understatement of the fucking year. I knew she wasn't ready to talk, but for her to just end things permanently? Yeah, I'm not taking this well. I've got a death grip on the table and I can feel what little control I have left slipping away. *What the fuck is she thinking?* I'm breathing like I'm on the verge of a fucking heart attack. Maybe I am.

"David, I need you to keep it together—at least until I can get us out of here."

Mike is standing next to me, trying to keep me from drawing any more attention to myself. Apparently, yelling the word "fuck" is frowned upon in establishments like this.

I manage to speak around my gritted teeth, "I'm fine. Don't I seem fine?"

He makes a noise that sounds suspiciously like laughter before throwing cash on the table and hauling my ass out of there. I suspect he flashed his badge at some point to keep everyone inside calm.

Once we reach my truck, he faces me. "Man, I know she picked a really shitty way of going about this, but you need to calm down and go talk to her."

My voice is cold when I respond, "Go talk to her? Really, Detective? That's the best idea you've got? I'm pretty sure that talking to me is the last thing she wants to do as she just had me served." I walk around him and climb into my truck.

"David—let's leave your truck here. Just come back to my place—"

I cut him off, "No, I don't want to be around anybody right now. I need a fuckin' minute, okay?"

Mike nods, his mouth a grim line, "Let me know if you change your mind."

I drive around aimlessly for hours. I can't believe it's come to this. I mean, I guess I should've seen it coming—we broke each other beyond repair. I guess I held onto this hope though that we could find our way back.

Everything was for her—the long nights in other towns and every back breaking second spent away from her. I did it all for her, but I lost sight of that. I didn't let her know that she was the most important thing and then I pushed having a kid on top of it. I should've listened to my dad. Just thinking of him dredges up a cesspool of memories and I don't want to face them right now.

After attending his funeral, I tried to go back to normal. I tried, but the weight of the fucking world was on my shoulders. I had to make sure my mom was okay while still running a business and being a husband. I fucked it up though. I put my wife last—when I did spend time at home (which was almost never), I hated her pitying glances. She was always checking in on me and I couldn't even tell her about the conversation my dad and I had the night

FORSAKING ALL OTHERS

before he died.

I finished up some jobs early one weekend and my mom was out of town staying with her sister. By all rights, my ass should've been home with my wife, but I didn't want to spend another weekend of tense silence and her walking around on eggshells. I drove back to town and found a local bar. I planned to drink until I could only remember the good stuff when Jess walked in. I was a bit surprised to see her out and about without Nate, especially considering that this bar wasn't in the best of neighborhoods.

Her eyes found mine almost immediately and she pulled up a chair next to me. I expected her to start talking, but she just sat silently as I ordered shot after shot.

Jess surprised me when she placed a hand on my thigh. She ran her hand back and forth lightly across the denim and I looked up, expecting to see pity. What I saw was lust. When she caught me staring at her, she bit down on her lower lip.

"Car. Now." I growled the words out, expecting her to slap me across the face and leave.

She grabbed her purse and leaned in next to my ear, "I brought my car. I'll drive us."

Like it was an everyday occurrence.

Once we got into her car, she started chattering away about finding a hotel room.

"No. Drive out of the city."

She looked upset, but drove us out into the country. I took her roughly in the backseat of her SUV and I didn't feel a damn thing.

I was numb.

When I finally showed up at the house the next day, I looked at Beth and willed myself to feel some emotion over what I'd done. Nothing.

It was like feeling required too much effort. I wish I could go back to the night she admitted she'd been taking birth control. I should've been man enough to accept her words for what they were—a sign that she was feeling alone. Instead I drove to the first bar I could find and drowned my sorrows in a bottle of whiskey, just as I had when my Dad died.

I wasn't even surprised to see Jess there this time. By the time she walked over, I was so far gone that the words just fell out of my mouth. I'd expected her to be shocked by Beth's behavior, but she said she knew and had tried to talk her out of it. Fuck, looking back on it, she told me everything I wanted to hear and I just ate it up.

When I stumbled out of that bar, I was beyond wasted. She took my keys and I briefly remember wondering how she was sober. She drove outside of town on some little deserted county road before putting the truck in park and climbing onto my lap.

By that point, I didn't give a flying fuck if either of us was married—I pulled the flimsy straps on her tank top down and took a nipple in my mouth while she worked on getting my jeans off. I can't remember a lot of the details after that.

All she talked about as she drove us back to the bar so she could get her car was how we were perfect for each other—shit I didn't take seriously at the time. I managed to make it home in one piece and I stood for several minutes outside the closed bedroom door, still too inebriated to feel any sense of remorse. I thought I was going to remain numb to my actions. I was wrong.

That next morning, I woke up in the guest room with a splitting headache and a strong urge to vomit when it hit me. I cheated. More than once. I cheated on a good woman who had done nothing but support my sorry ass while I got my business off the ground. I couldn't speak to her, I was so scared I'd lose my shit and break down in front of her.

The guilt was all encompassing. It was this weight on me. I wanted to throw myself at her feet and confess every sin before begging for her mercy and forgiveness. I couldn't do that to her though, so I kept my mouth shut. Beth took my silence as a sign I was still angry at her and when she blinked rapidly and turned away, it was like someone ripped my fucking heart out of my chest. My emotions decided to return with vengeance. I bought the tickets to Mexico without a second thought. I wanted me and her alone on a beach—I guess I thought we'd reconnect and it'd be like it never happened. The truth always has a way of coming out though.

The third and last time was when I was working out of town. I heard a knock on my hotel room door late one evening and she was there. I don't even know how she tracked me down. I'd had a few drinks at dinner, so I was feeling a nice buzz. I had her up against the wall with my hand on her throat. I'd dodged her text messages after Nate left and I was so fucking pissed that she had shown up. I took my frustration out on her body. It wasn't like I was in love with her, hell I didn't even like her the majority of the time. One thing I am damn sure of is that I had a condom on when I slipped inside of her, just as I had the previous times.

My phone rang afterward while Jess was in the bathroom. It was Beth and she sounded scared. When she admitted that someone had broken into the house, I knew it had to end. I had to be the kind of husband my dad was for my mom. I owed it to him. Shit, we were trying to have a kid. When Beth and I hung up, I started tossing all my shit into a bag. Jess walked out of the bathroom with just a towel wrapped around her and I tossed her clothes at her. "Get your clothes on and leave. We're done here."

She tried arguing with me, but I wouldn't hear it. What we had done to Beth was unforgivable and I didn't know how, but I would make it up to her—even if it took me the rest of my life.

I glance down at the clock and see that it's still early—I bet the liquor store is open. I can't deal with this sober.

CHAPTER FIVE

Beth

I'm pregnant. I lie in bed and stroke my flat belly with the palm of my hand. I can't believe it. I'm still trying to figure out who I was before the accident and now I'm going to be responsible for another person? I don't know that I've ever been as scared as I am right now.

I mean how do single parents do it? Financially, I can barely afford to cover myself and the thought of paying for diapers and daycare is enough to send my pulse racing. *I wonder if the baby will have his blue eyes.* The thought startles me.

David.

My Achilles heel.

I am not certain of a lot of things right now, but the way I feel about him is a done deal. I love him with every fiber of my being, but his betrayal has cut me to the bone. The floodgate of memories of my life with him turned lust into love. I didn't want to file for divorce, but how could I ever look at him again without imagining him with Jess? How could he look at me and not see me with Landon?

It's like when you break a glass. You might be able to super glue the pieces back together, but you'll still be able to see the cracks from where everything splintered apart.

I lie in the dark with the moonlight streaming in from the window above the bed. It feels like hours that I've been left alone, stray thoughts running rampant through my head.

Landon.

I haven't heard from him since that night and I feel as though there's still a lot to process as far as memories go.

It's incredibly frustrating being locked outside of your own memories. I gained quite a few when Landon showed up six weeks ago, but there's this nagging feeling that I'm still missing something crucial.

Lauren seemed patient enough at first to answer my unending questions, but I think even she's run out of answers for me. I'm on my own.

Despite my best efforts, my body gives in to sleep.

As I choke down a piece of dry toast the next morning, I decide to research pregnancy so I know what's to come. I Google the word and I'm visually assaulted with site after site, each proclaiming to be the web's leader in pregnancy and childbirth, whatever the hell that means.

I click on one at random and it immediately asks for the first day of my last period or the date I conceived. I don't see an option labeled, *"I was just involved in a serious car wreck and suffered amnesia, so your guess is as good as mine."*

I know I wasn't pregnant right after the wreck. The emergency room doctors ran lab-work for that. I grab the calendar off the desk and flip back to June.

The wreck was the night of June twelfth and I didn't leave the hospital until June sixteenth.

Possible conception dates...

FORSAKING ALL OTHERS

Well, we didn't waste any time once we got home—looks like the lucky dates are either June sixteenth or seventeenth.

I type in June sixteenth and a blue box pops up. ***"Congratulations, Mommy! Your baby's due date is March 9th, 2015."***

I'm eight weeks along according to the website's charts and I could've had a positive pregnancy test as early as June thirtieth.

Eight weeks!

June thirtieth!

What in the hell have I been doing for the last six weeks? How did I miss this?

It's almost August and I've been carrying this little person around for the last six weeks without knowing.

I begin clicking at random and a video pops up of what appear to be the cursed mer-people from *The Little Mermaid.*

Apparently, it's meant to be a video of what my baby looks like at this stage. The baby is half an inch long and growing its arms and legs.

I choke back tears as I watch the computer animated embryo dance around on the screen.

We made that.

Regardless of all the shit, he and I were perfect together in that moment and we made this.

If only he hadn't done the same thing with my former best friend.

CHAPTER SIX
David

The alarm clock won't stop its shrill ringing. I roll over and try to use my hand and feel for it.

"Beth, turn off your alarm." I mumble the words before realizing I'm not at home and my wife hasn't been in my bed for over six weeks now.

I finally locate the clock and mash every button on it, but the ringing won't stop. My head is pounding and my mouth feels like cotton. I don't even know if I'm hungover or still drunk from the night before. It's hard to keep track. I've been drinking like this since I was served divorce papers.

Come to think of it, I don't know if I've sobered up enough long enough to experience a true hangover.

The ringing stops and then immediately starts up again. It's my fucking phone.

I keep my eyes closed and press it against my ear. "Hello?" My voice sounds like a rusted gate, as though it hasn't been used in a while.

"Where the hell are you?" The female voice is definitely not my wife's. "You were supposed to be here fifteen minutes ago, or did you forget that you agreed to come to this doctor visit with me?"

I sigh, "Jess, I—shit, I'll be there in ten."

I end the call and finally open my eyes to the destruction before me. There are empty glass bottles everywhere and a chair is on its side. I mean, this hotel room wasn't five-star to begin with, but this is something else entirely.

You have got to get your shit together, man.

I sidestep the warzone that is the hotel floor and make my way into the bathroom to splash cold water on my face. I need a shower, but I don't have the time for it.

My eyes are bloodshot. I look like death warmed over. My beard is poking out in every direction—I look like a bear that missed out on hibernation. As I grab my toothbrush, I can hear Beth lecturing me about the importance of good oral hygiene. God, all these little reminders of her are going to be the death of me.

I walk into the medical building and find Jess sitting in the corner of the waiting room, texting like her life depends on it. I go over and take a seat across from her.

"You're late." She doesn't even bother looking up from her phone.

"Looks like you're still sitting in the waiting room, so I can't be that late."

She looks up long enough to roll her eyes at me before going back to her phone.

Fine with me. We can sit in silence for the entire appointment.

I study her as she continues to tap out texts on her phone. She's the anti-Beth in every way. She may possess that long and lean look that women everywhere go crazy trying to achieve, but I'm a man. I love that my wife is so tiny when standing next to me and the fact that she has curves for days has never hurt either.

God, I miss her.

Jess notices me staring at her and mistakes it for attraction. She pouts her lower lip out, "I know you feel bad about being late so

I'll let you make it up to me later." She winks and I resist the urge to hurl onto her expensive heels.

I ignore her comment and begin checking work emails.

We are a match made in Hell.

I'm responding to a request for a bid when I hear it.

"Mrs. Greene if you'll just wait right in here, they'll call you back shortly."

My head pops up and I begin searching the room. The nurse is blocking my view, but I know it's her. I feel it.

When the nurse walks out, I watch Beth set her purse down while she searches for a magazine and my heart is ready to fucking beat out of my chest.

She looks absolutely beautiful. She's wearing a simple sundress and flip flops and her unruly blonde hair is piled up on top of her head. I wonder what she'd do if I walked over and freed it from the messy bun she's confined it in. I just want to run my rough hands through it.

Would she fight me if I took her bottom lip in my mouth? I could carry her right out of here and back to the house...

I don't even realize I'm leaning forward until Jess kicks me with her heel. "You wanna respect the woman you're here with, or are you picking out your next conquest, Romeo?" She follows my gaze and I take pleasure in watching the color drain from her face when she sees that it's Beth.

"What is she doing here?"

I pause at her question. *What is she doing here?* I'm on my feet and walking towards her before I even stop to think of the consequences.

"David!" Jess hisses after me.

"Beth?"

She starts at the sound of my voice and turns away from the magazine rack slowly. "David?" Her eyes widen, "How did you know where I'd be?"

I swallow, "I'm uh actually here with—" I gesture toward Jess, who is shooting daggers at me with her eyes.

I watch as her shoulders drop, she's disappointed. "Of course." I hear her mutter under her breath, "Stupid, Beth."

"Why are you here? Are you?—" I don't quite know how to finish that sentence.

She shakes her head rapidly, "No. Just my annual check-up."

I'm crushed. How fucked up is that? I'm expecting a baby with Jess, and in this moment, I wish more than anything that it was with her.

She gestures to her magazine, "Well, I'm gonna go sit down. Take care, David." She turns away and goes back to her seat.

I stare dumbly at her. *Take care?* That's it? Like we're nothing more than two strangers meeting on the street. I'm about to take her by the arm and find somewhere a little more private to discuss this when Jess's shrill voice rings out across the room.

"David? They're ready for us, honey!"

Beth looks up from her magazine and her skin appears to have taken on a greenish hue.

Jess just can't help herself without getting a little dig in by pretending we're a couple.

"Beth? You okay?"

She nods and waves me off, but I see a lone tear running down her cheek before I turn back to Jess.

I don't think there's been a moment, up until this point, where I've felt this low.

Once we reach the back, the same nurse we always see tells

Jess to put a gown on. I'm finally going to be present for an ultrasound. I've played along with the charade of concerned partner, but I need visual proof. Hell, I need more than visual proof.

I stop the nurse before she steps out. "Is she far enough along to determine paternity?"

Jess makes a cry of outrage and the nurse gives me a death look.

"I know you can do a blood test on her after the eighth week and it determines paternity—"

"David, where is this coming from? You know it's yours!" She attempts to place her hand on my arm and I shrug her off.

"Surprised that I did more than just drink when you told me? I know that it's accurate and safe and I want the damn thing done today. You've gotta be what— fifteen or sixteen weeks by now?" I spit the words out as though they're venom.

She opens and closes her mouth and I can see that she is trying to think of a reason why she can't submit to the test.

It's the closest I'm getting to an answer and without another look, I turn around and walk out.

"David!" Jess comes after me using the gown to cover herself, "Wait a second. I'll do the testing, I just wasn't prepared for you to ask."

"Jess, I've waited long enough for answers—" The nurse walks out into the hall and I look past Jess, "You heard her. She consents. I want that test ordered."

CHAPTER SEVEN

Beth

Seeing him did more than cut my heart. It made ribbons out of it. With my head down, I mindlessly thumb through a women's magazine, silently willing the tears to stop.

I know it's stupid, but for a split second, when I saw him standing there—I thought he was there for me. And in that moment, I was ready to throw myself on him and tell him the divorce papers were a mistake. That wouldn't have been a desperate move...nope, not one bit. My inner romantic is so worked up, she's breathing into a paper bag.

"Elizabeth Greene?"

I look up at the nurse who is scanning the crowded waiting room, obviously searching for me.

I grab my purse and try to put thoughts of hooking up with my soon-to-be ex-husband out of my head. *What the hell is wrong with me?*

Once we arrive in the back, the nurse has me set my things down so she can check my weight. I wince, afraid to see how much I've already gained. The number I see shocks me though. I've lost weight, a lot of it. I'm fifteen pounds lighter than I was in the hospital right after the wreck.

The nurse enters the information into her computer, seemingly unconcerned by this development.

I clear my throat, "Um, excuse me? Is this scale accurate?

Because my weight is a lot lower than normal and with me being," I make a gesture of a round belly. I don't know why I'm now unable to say the word "pregnant."

She looks bemused, "Have you been experiencing a lot of morning sickness?"

"You mean, 'all day sickness?' Yeah, lots of that happening over here."

She laughs, "I'll let Dr. Harper know. She might be able to prescribe you something to help alleviate some of that."

After going over any questions I might have for Dr. Harper, she hands me a gown and leaves the room so that I can change. I change and try to get comfortable on the exam table. The paper lining on the table crinkles under me as I try to get comfortable. It's then that I fully notice the pictures lining the wall in front of me. Babies.

The babies all appear to be newborns and they are in the most adorable poses. One is dressed like a little fairy, she's even got a wand in her hand. Another is wearing a teeny-tiny football jersey and is sleeping inside a football helmet. I find that I've been absentmindedly stroking my stomach while lost in thoughts of infant photography. *I need the name of this photographer.* An emotion I don't quite recognize comes over me just as Dr. Harper comes in.

"Good mornin' Elizabeth, and congratulations!"

"So, it's real. I'm really pregnant?" I smile as I say the words.

"Yes ma'am. The lab work and urine sample both confirmed that you are indeed pregnant. Your hCG levels place you around seven to eight weeks, but I'm going to confirm that with an ultrasound."

"You mean I'll get to see my baby today?"

"I'm going to do a pelvic exam and then we'll see what's going on."

She does her exam, while asking me questions regarding diseases that may run in our family. I answer her questions as best I can, but I'll have to figure out a way to find out more from David's side of the family.

She finishes up and a nurse wheels a cart into the room and begins placing what looks like a condom on the wand connected to the machine. I am trying to figure out why they need a condom on something they're putting on my belly when Dr. Harper sees my face.

"Elizabeth, you're not far enough along for us to do a normal ultrasound on you, so we're going to do a transvaginal one instead."

My eyes must be as wide as saucers, "Okay, great," I manage to squeak out.

There is so much I don't know about all of this. The nurse squirts lube onto the wand and has me lie back. I focus on the little screen and not the fact that the most action I've had in six weeks is coming to me courtesy of an ultrasound wand.

The black and white screen is empty one second and then there it is. It looks like a gummy bear and it's moving around like crazy. There's also a sound like a washer on spin cycle.

Dr. Harper smiles at me, "You hear your baby's heartbeat? We should be able to get it with the Doppler at your next visit."

I nod and place my hand over my mouth, completely overcome with emotion at the sweet little creature grooving on the monitor. The thought that David is in a nearby exam room, doing this very same thing with Jess, brings me back to reality.

They print out pictures for me to take home and slightly dazed,

I head for the elevators after making my next appointment. If I were paying more attention, I wouldn't have run smack dab into my former best friend.

I apologize for bumping into the woman before realizing it's Jess. She tries to hug me and I step to the side, avoiding her at all costs.

"Lizzie. God, I am so sorry." Gone is the cool, calm, and collected Jess who couldn't be bothered to walk over to me in the waiting room. In her place is a nervous and weepy mess. I think of that song by Gotye and realize how true his words were in that song. She is nothing more than somebody I used to know.

I walk over to the other elevator and push the down arrow, willing the doors to open soon. Never mind that it's already lit up. Maybe if I push it a few more times, it'll come quicker. She places her hand on my arm and I tense up, ready to lay into her. *Stress isn't good for the baby.* I take a deep breath and try to clear my mind. It's funny, but I haven't had a panic attack since that night, and I refuse to have one in front of the elevators at my doctor's office.

I keep my voice calm, "Not here, Jess. I have nothing to say to you. You got him—and I'd really appreciate it if you could just leave me the fuck alone now."

She starts openly weeping again, but I refuse to look at her, instead focusing on the metallic elevator doors.

Her voice cuts through the tears, "I never wanted to hurt you. I didn't want it to affect us. I just—"

Forgetting that I was not going to engage her, I turn towards her and unleash my fury. "You just what, Jess? Thought you and I could remain friends while you slept with him? We aren't sister wives—this isn't some normal thing between friends!"

FORSAKING ALL OTHERS

The elevator doors pop open at that moment and as I step in, I see quite a few shocked faces staring back. I hit the button to close the doors and focus on my breathing again. "Sorry, little bean," I rub my stomach. I need to remain stress free and probably eat more vegetables while I'm at it—growing a little human is hard work.

I've just made it to my car when my "sister wives" comment hits me and I cannot help myself, I double over in laughter. My head against the driver side window, I laugh until I'm crying. These pregnancy hormones are out of control right now.

"Elizabeth."

His voice effectively stops any sort of outburst from me.

I turn to look at him, standing with his hands in his pockets, waiting for me to say something.

"Landon—what are you doing here?"

He gestures toward the large building behind me, "I had an appointment. What are you doing here?"

"Same, actually."

"You seem upset. Bad news?"

He's fishing for information and while a part of me remembers how caring he was toward me when David wasn't around, a larger part of me is very much on guard.

"No—nothing like that. Just being emotional." I wave my hand as I speak as though that will better illustrate my point.

He runs his hand through his hair, seemingly at a loss for words. I've just opened the door when he regains it. "Coffee. I mean—do you want to grab coffee? There's a place nearby."

The thought of trying to ingest anything at the moment makes my stomach turn. "I've actually got to get back to work. Maybe another time."

He nods sadly and I turn back toward my car.

"I saw, Elizabeth."

I freeze, all too aware of the sonogram pictures in my purse. *How did he find out?*

Seeing my wide eyes, he clarifies, 'It was in the paper."

My heart is pounding so hard, I fear it may come right out of my chest. "It was in the paper? Why?"

"It's public record." He's looking at me like I've lost my head.

Public record. Public recor—the divorce.

I let out a breath, "The divorce. You're talking about the divorce."

"What else would I be talking about?"

I laugh shakily. *Think, Elizabeth, think.* "I thought you meant the whole 'me having an affair while he was having an affair' thing."

He laughs easily, "I don't think that makes the paper unless you're a celebrity. I thought you might want a friend to talk to during this time."

I suddenly became interested in asphalt underneath my feet.

"Landon—"

He interrupts me, "Look, I get it. You've got a lot to sort through," He touches my arm, "Just know that I'm going to be here—waiting for you whenever you're ready."

I mutter a quick thanks before jumping into my car. *Why am I so awkward around him?*

CHAPTER EIGHT

David

I've been sitting in my truck for the last half hour, making calls and answering emails. I've tried to do anything, but think about what just went down with Jess. I feel like I'm fucking up at every turn. I've just finished up a call on my current job site when I see Beth come out of the medical building.

The breeze catches the little strands of her hair that aren't pinned up, and I'm fucking mesmerized by it. I had to park in the lot across the street so I've got a great vantage point. I can see her and make sure she gets to her car safely, but she can't see me.

I watch as she gets to her SUV and dissolves into full-blown laughter. She's leaning her head against the window and I wonder what the hell happened in there. I'm just as thrown when her laughter suddenly switches over to tears and without a thought, I'm out of my truck headed her way when Landon pops up behind her.

What the fuck? Is he stalking her?

I'm ready to interrupt when I see her facial expression change. *She's afraid of him.* I know my wife, inside and out, and her eyes always give her thoughts away. I don't want to rush in to the situation and face her wrath, but I want to be nearby in case she needs me.

They continue talking for a few minutes before Beth climbs into her SUV and leaves. Landon watches her drive away before heading to his vehicle. I'm tempted to confront him, but I need to be patient. I'm going to need concrete evidence before taking him down.

I make it through the workday, in spite of the thoughts of Beth spinning in my head. I've yet to discuss the divorce with her, but as I leave the last jobsite, I think that conversation is overdue. I'm not a passive man, so I'll be damned if I just cave and agree to divorce. She and I messed up—there's got to be a way that we can come back from it though. Blake Shelton comes on the radio and it damn near breaks me. It's like he's singing about the situation I'm in, if I'd done more to show her how important she was to me, maybe she wouldn't be gone.

Once I get to the house, I try to get my emotions under control. I can't go in there guns blazing and demand that she take me back. I'll be out on my ass before I even get the words out. No, I can't lose my temper. I did that in those first few weeks after she kicked me out and I got a door to the face each time.

I knock on the front door of my own house and I find it slightly amusing that my heart is beating just as fast as the first time I went to pick her up for a date. She still has this effect on me, I just took it for granted before.

Beth opens the front door and I'm blown away just by the sight of her. Her unruly hair is finally down and she's just in a tank top and shorts. *I want her so badly.*

"David? What are you doing here?"

"I needed to see you. We didn't get a chance to discuss much earlier. I want to talk about the divorce." I've succeeded in keeping my voice calm, even though the anger is bubbling just under the surface.

"Okay." She gives me a resigned look and holds the door open for me to come in. She isn't throwing it shut in my face, so I'd say we're making progress.

I look around our house and notice boxes sitting on almost every available surface. "What the hell is this?" I gesture at them with my hand. Okay, anger is definitely becoming more pronounced.

She looks up at me from where she's sitting in her chair. Her face is the picture of innocence, but her eyes blaze at my tone. "I'm moving, David."

I sigh, "Is this because of the divorce papers, because I'm not fucking signing them. We were good together and we could be good together again."

She laughs and it takes me by surprise. "Good together? You mean when we were cheating on each other? Is that the definition of a good marriage to you? Geez, you think that's how it was for your parents?" The venom in her words is enough to bring the rage I feel at this entire situation to the forefront.

I snarl, "Do not bring my parents into this. Answer the damn question. Why are you moving?"

She jumps up off the chair and comes to stand directly in front of me. Looks like I just lit her fuse. *So much for a productive conversation.*

"Look around you, David. There are reminders of us everywhere in this house. I know that you're living in a hotel right now—it's just not right. Not when you're expecting a baby with her," her face puckers as she says the word 'baby' and I'm afraid she's going to be sick, but she stoically continues, "I'm thinking of moving in with Lauren, she needs a roommate. I thought you'd want to be a family, and I know Jess won't stand for living anywhere but here."

"Fuck Jess!" I don't mean to shout the words but I do.

Beth leans over, clutching her knees, her shoulders heaving. I've done it. Now, she's crying. I place my hand on her shoulder just as she pops her head up, I narrowly avoid getting my nose broken. She's got tears running down her face, but she is laughing! Laughing at what, I have no idea. "What's so funny?"

She catches her breath long enough to enlighten me. "Fuck Jess? Didn't you already do that, David?"

She immediately begins wheezing with laughter again and I worry she's lost it. All the stress from the accident and finding out about the infidelity has done it. She's snapped.

"Are you okay, Beth?"

She straightens up, wiping tears away with the back of her hand. "I'm fine, David. I'm just trying to add some humor to all of this."

I take a step toward her and she backs up. I continue doing so until her back hits the living room wall. I cage her in, my arms on either side of her head. "Beth, none of this is funny—" I plan to say more, but her heaving chest and wide eyes take me under. She's staring up at me, waiting to see what I do next.

I lean down and press my lips to hers. She's so soft and sweet. I nip at her lower lip, drawing her in further. I'm a selfish bastard, I know that. I should let her go and maybe later, once I've had a few drinks, I'll agree to do just that. At this moment though, I'm going to savor the feel and taste of her.

I expect her to stop me when she brings her hands up, but she surprises me. Her hands lock around my waist, pulling me even closer to her. *If she's gone mad, I don't know that I want her to regain sanity.* My tongue makes its way inside her sweet mouth and I feel that I am quickly losing control.

I pull away reluctantly, "Beth—I gotta stop," her face falls, "Baby, if we don't stop, I'm going to pick you up and we're going to bed. Believe me, I'd love nothing more, but I want us to talk. I need to know why you filed."

Beth bites her bottom lip, which is swollen from my assault on her mouth. "David, I didn't know what else to do. We hurt each other badly and obviously we weren't enough for each other," she hesitates and her voice is almost too quiet to hear, "More than that though—I can't help raise a child that you and Jess made. It would be this forever reminder every time I looked at him or her."

Her words crush me. I knew the situation would be hard to manage, but I never looked at it from her standpoint. Raising a child that was the product of infidelity—I don't know that a saint would take that on. I run my hands over my eyes, as if that will give me a clear mind. Instead, it dredges up anger again.

"What about Landon? I saw you two today in the parking lot. Are you going to start seeing him?"

She glares at me, "First of all, that's not any of your concern and secondly, why were you staking out the office parking lot?"

"I wasn't staking out the parking lot, but I do find it interesting that Landon just so happened to be there today. I don't trust the guy. I think he's stalking you."

She laughs without humor, "That's interesting, coming from the guy who was camped out in the same parking lot, watching me."

"I saw the way he looked at you, Beth. Jesus, you think I'm just going to consent to a divorce so you'll be free to go to him?"

"You have no right to contest this, David. No right!"

The anger has now taken over, "That's where you're wrong. I have every goddamn right. You are my wife! I fucked up, I'm well aware, but I'll be damned if I let you go without a fight!"

She's crying now and I feel like the world's biggest asshole. Her voice is just above a whisper due to her tears, "Please, David. Please don't make me relive it. I don't want to see Jess every time I look at you—just like you don't want to look at me and see Landon. We're poison to each other, you and me."

Her words are like a knife to my chest. "Beth, I love you. I love you so damn much and I'm not signing the papers. I've got sixty days, the way I see it. Sixty days to make you see what a mistake this is."

She sinks down the wall until she's sitting, "You're really going to fight me? You want to go before a judge to settle this?"

I nod, "If that's what it takes. In the meantime, be prepared to see a lot of me, baby. Because I'm not going anywhere."

"Get out, David."

I push the anger down and try to lighten the mood, "So, I guess you're taking a raincheck on sex tonight or is that still on the table?"

Her mouth falls open in shock and I grin at her, even though smiling is the last thing I feel like doing. "Should I alert the media that I've rendered Beth Greene speechless?"

She frowns at me, but her gaze is heated and I know I've gotten through to her, at least physically. "Good night, David. Don't let the door hit you in the ass on your way out."

When I get back to the hotel, I immediately reach for the bottle of Pendleton. I'm ready to get lost in the bottle when I think of her words. *I've got to change.* I can't numb myself to this anymore. As much as it's going to suck, I need sobriety to fix all of this and get her back. I dump the rest of the bottle down the bathroom sink and prepare for the hangover from fucking hell.

CHAPTER NINE
Beth

It's been a long, emotionally exhausting day. I thought seeing Jess and David was stressful enough, but then Landon popped up by my car. It would be a severe understatement to say that I was emotionally tapped out by the time I managed to get into my car to leave. Of course, because it's my life, it couldn't end there. Fate couldn't let me enjoy the rest of my day in peace, no sir.

I'd just about gotten my blood pressure back into a normal range and was jamming out to some Taylor Swift on the radio when it happened. The music cut off abruptly due to an incoming call…from my mother. You know, after the car wreck, she made no attempt to reach out to me. Maybe I deserved that, I had thrown her under a bus to keep my sins a secret after all. On the other hand, it was like a breath of fresh air to not have my every move scrutinized.

"Hi Mom." I answer with a cheeriness that I certainly do not feel.

"Elizabeth. I was working in the front flower bed this morning when Jean stopped by with the newspaper. Would you like to guess what she showed me?" Her tone is clipped and I feel as though I'm back to being eight years-old, scolded for breaking a piece of china.

"I can't imagine what it could be, mother." She hasn't bothered to pick up a phone and check on me in over six weeks. I'm not giving her what she wants that easily.

There's silence for a couple of seconds and then my mother shrieks into the phone, "Do not play games with me, Elizabeth Marie! You filed for divorce from David?

I have to turn the car's volume down in an effort to save what's left of my hearing.

"Oh, that. Yeah, I filed for divorce." *I'm going straight to Hell.*

"Why? Why in God's name would you throw away a marriage to a man who has put up with so much from you? Is this because of that other guy? Are you divorcing David to be with him? I raised you better than this, Elizabeth!"

Because I have no shame at this point, I begin laughing and it takes me a minute to collect myself so that I can answer her. "No, I am not divorcing David so that I can be with 'that other guy.' It just didn't work out."

I debate on whether or not to tell her the truth, but then I remember, again, that this is the same woman who couldn't be bothered to see if her only child was okay after the car accident. Even her busybody of a best friend, Jean, at least sent flowers.

"I don't recognize you anymore, Elizabeth. This behavior is too much. And what will people think when they find out? This—"

I cut her off with what sounds very much like a snarl, "You don't recognize me? That's fanfuckingtastic! You wanna know why? Because I don't recognize myself anymore. That girl who was afraid of everything? Yeah, she died in that car wreck. Which car wreck, you ask? The one that almost killed me, mother! You wouldn't know because you couldn't be bothered to check in," I suck in a deep breath in order to continue, "And seriously, who gives a flying fuck what other people think? They're certainly not the ones having to live through it. I'm so sorry to have made you look bad in front of your uppity church friends, but I'll be damned if I let you speak to me like this ever again."

I hear her sharp intake of breath before smashing the end call button with a little more force than was probably necessary.

My pulse is racing and my body feels as though it's experiencing fight or flight. "I'm sorry, little bean. I'm so sorry. I shouldn't get upset like that—it's no good for you." I don't know why I've adopted the nickname, "bean," but it fits.

I'm traumatizing this baby already. The amount of stress this poor thing has been subjected to just in the last hour has me ready to turn the car around and drive back to my doctor's office.

The tears fall silently onto my lap for the remainder of my drive back to work.

When I get home, I immediately strip out of my work clothes and let my hair down—literally. I want nothing more than to climb into bed and sleep. It doesn't matter how much sleep I get lately, it never seems to be enough. Every ounce of energy is being poured into growing this baby and I'm running on fumes right now.

I pull out my ultrasound pictures and settle in to bed, studying every little feature of my gummy bear. I'd been feeling like I was spinning out of control, but the minute I heard the heartbeat and saw it dancing around on the ultrasound screen, I was in love. In that moment, I knew that every part of this journey was worth it. The daily vomiting, needing a nap at lunchtime every day, and generally just being an emotional wreck—I'd gladly bear this cross in order to bring the best part of me and David into this world. *I mean, I'd prefer that the vomiting stop sooner rather than later, to be honest.*

FORSAKING ALL OTHERS

The knock at the door interrupts my thoughts. I'm a bit wary when it comes to answering doors lately—especially when I'm not expecting company.

I open the door up to find David leaning against the bricks of the house. He's wearing a fitted black t-shirt and jeans that hug his lower body. His hair is windblown and it's obvious he's come straight from work. I tried not to let myself notice him this morning, but now I have to pull my gaze away from him. My inner romantic is shaving her legs and touching up her makeup.

"David? What are you doing here?"

"I needed to see you. We didn't get a chance to discuss much earlier. I want to talk about the divorce."

The divorce. It's really the last thing I want to discuss right now, but I feel like I've talked it over with everyone else today—what's one more person?

I take a deep breath and let it out slowly. "Okay." I hold the door for him and try to keep my gaze passive.

He immediately notices the plethora of boxes I've got scattered throughout the living room. His face immediately darkens. *Shit, looks like nice David has left the building.*

"What the hell is this?"

"I'm moving, David." I don't know why he looks surprised by this.

He sighs, "Is this because of the divorce papers, because I'm not fucking signing them. We were good together and we could be good together again."

I immediately begin laughing. This has been the most emotionally exhausting day and the fact that he thinks we can come back from this is suddenly hilarious to me. "Good together? You mean when we were cheating on each other? Is that the definition of a good marriage to you? Geez, you think that's how it was for your parents?" I don't mean to hit below the belt with my comment, but someone has to bring rationality back to the conversation. David's dad, John, was an amazing husband and father. I can't imagine that he and Louisa ever had to navigate a situation like this.

"Do not bring my parents into this. Answer the damn question. Why are you moving?"

So much for being comfortable. I will not sit here and let him yell at me like I'm a child. I get out of my chair and stand before him, daring him to push me any further. "Look around you, David. There are reminders of us everywhere in this house. I know you're living in a hotel right now—it's just not right. Not when you're expecting a baby with her," the bile rises in my throat. When will I be able to discuss the two of them procreating without barfing? "I'm thinking of moving in with Lauren, she needs a roommate. I thought you'd want to be a family, and I know Jess won't stand for living anywhere but here."

His voice is so loud, it startles me. "Fuck Jess!"

I can't help it. I lean over and lose myself in silent laughter. Tears are pouring from my eyes. Out of all the things he could've said, I did not expect that. I also didn't expect to have such a visceral reaction when his hand touches my shoulder. It reminds me of a song by Frou Frou. I feel that I could "ride a wave" from David's inhaling, exhaling—probably even him just standing in front of me. *Damn pregnancy hormones.*

"What's so funny?" He doesn't sound amused.

It takes me a minute to get myself under control long enough to tell him. "Fuck Jess? Didn't you already do that, David?" I fall apart again and I think I've snorted at least twice during my laughing fit. *So ladylike.*

He takes his hand off my shoulder. "Are you okay, Beth?"

I stand back up, trying to compose myself. "I'm fine, David. I'm just trying to add some humor to all of this."

David looks pissed. He take a step toward me and I instinctively take a step back. My heart is going double time and my desire for him is like a forest fire—raging out of control. *Lord help me.*

He backs me into a wall and cages me in his arms. I look up at him, willing him with my mind. *Kiss me. Kiss me. For the love of God, kiss me.* It's become a chant that I'm repeating over and over.

"Beth, none of this is funny—"

He's right. Nothing about this is funny or cute. I've just filed for divorce and now I'm silently begging him to kiss me. Maybe he's right to worry about my mental state. I've obviously lost my damn—

His mouth is on mine before I can finish my thought and I am ready to forget everything. The divorce. Jess. Their baby. We could run away, live on an island somewhere. He could fish for a living and I could open a little beachside café for tourists. We'd be so happy. Just us and our little bean.

Yeah, Rationality? It was nice of you to stop by, but I'm gonna need you to leave now.

I bring my hands up and wrap them around his waist, pulling his strong body into mine. He smells like sawdust and sweat. Incredibly, I find that turns me on even more. I need this contact. I'm all but grinding myself against him when he pulls away from me.

"Beth—I gotta stop," *No! We can't stop now!* "Baby, if we don't stop, I'm going to pick you up and we're going to bed.

Believe me, I'd love nothing more, but I want us to talk. I need to know why you filed."

I bite my lip, stalling for time. I'm trying to hold onto this high, but his words are sending me crashing back to earth. "David, I didn't know what else to do. We hurt each other badly and obviously we weren't enough for each other," I stop myself. I don't want to fight with him, especially since we were just getting along so well, "More than that though—I can't help raise a child that you and Jess made. It would be this forever reminder every time I looked at him or her."

He runs his hands over his eyes and I know he's trying to keep his temper in check. The thought surprises me. Just when I feel that I've remembered everything, little things like this come back to me from out of the blue.

"What about Landon? I saw you two today in the parking lot. Are you going to start seeing him?"

What? How would he know that?

"First of all that is not any of your concern and secondly, why were you staking out the office parking lot?"

He's getting frustrated and he has no trouble letting me know it. "I wasn't staking out the parking lot, but I do find it interesting that Landon just so happened to be there today. I don't trust the guy. I think he's stalking you."

I laugh mirthlessly, "That's interesting, coming from the guy who was camped out in the same parking lot, watching me."

Oh, hello pot. Meet the kettle.

"I saw the way he looked at you, Beth. Jesus, you think I'm just going to consent to a divorce so you'll be free to go to him?"

My inner romantic is searching for migraine medicine at this point. Way to kill the mood.

FORSAKING ALL OTHERS

Deep breaths. In and out. In and—oh fuck it.

"You have no right to contest this, David. No right!"

He slams his hand down on the table next to the sofa. "That's where you're wrong. I have every goddamn right. You are my wife! I fucked up, I'm well aware, but I'll be damned if I let you go without a fight!"

And right on cue, here come the waterworks. Why can't I just be angry? Why do I have to cry? I need to end this fight now. I don't have any energy left to expend here.

My voice comes out much softer than I anticipated, "Please, David. Please don't make me relive it. I don't want to see Jess every time I look at you—just like you don't want to look at me and see Landon. We're poison to each other, you and me."

He moves around behind the sofa, and I'm not sure if he's aware that he's just placed a barrier between us.

"Beth, I love you. I love you so damn much and I'm not signing the papers. I've got sixty days, the way I see it. Sixty days to make you see what a mistake this is."

Damn. He's been doing his research. The sadistic side of me thought he'd sign the papers and run off to start a new life with Jess. My inner romantic hoped he'd do exactly what he's doing now. To say I'm experiencing internal conflict would be putting it mildly.

I sit down on the floor, my legs suddenly refusing to cooperate anymore. "You're really going to fight me? You want to go before a judge to settle this?"

Please say yes. *What? No. I meant please say no.*

He nods at me, "If that's what it takes. In the meantime, be prepared to see a lot of me, baby. Because I'm not going anywhere."

I can't think straight anymore. My head is swimming in anger and lust. "Get out, David."

The fight goes out of his eyes and I breathe a sigh of relief. I can't handle any more drama today.

"So, I guess you're taking a raincheck on sex tonight or is that still on the table?"

My inner romantic peeks out from behind the bedroom door. I cannot help it. His comment is so out of left field that my mouth hangs open and I can't find the words.

He smiles at me, the cocky son-of-a-bitch. "Should I alert the media that I've rendered Beth Greene speechless?"

He's still leaning across the back of the sofa and I'm mentally cursing it for blocking my view of his body. Not that I'm going to cave in to his demands, I just want to see the effect this conversation is having on him. That's it. It's purely for research purposes.

I frown at him so he knows I mean business, "Good night, David. Don't let the door hit you in the ass on your way out."

My phone rings less than a minute after he leaves. I answer with a groan, "David. I can't talk to you right now. I already told–"

Lauren's laugh travels through the phone. "You do realize it's 2014 don't you? I mean technology has come a long way. We have this new thing known as caller ID. It actually shows you who is calling. All you have to do is look at your screen and voilà."

I groan, "Okay, smartass. I get it. Why are you calling?"

Her voice gets higher, "I just wanted to check in on you. Maybe I'm in the neighborhood and wanted to stop by."

I go to take off my glasses so I can rub my eyes before realizing I made myself wear contacts today.

"Why are you lying? Did he call you? Tell you I needed

company?"

"Well, in the year of our Lord, two thousand fourteen, we also have this newfangled technology that allows us to send mini emails directly to another person's phone. They call it texting. Silly me, I didn't clarify what emails are. When—"

I interrupt her technology rant, "I get it. Just come over. I don't care anymore!" I say the last part with laughter though.

CHAPTER TEN
Beth

Lauren arrives within five minutes carrying a couple of grocery bags. She pulls out ice cream, yogurt, milk, and four different packages of cheese. There's sliced cheese, cubed cheese, a wedge of cheese, and even shredded cheese.

I look at her questioningly. "Laur—what is all this?"

She grins proudly, "I've been doing my research into this pregnancy business. And, calcium is extremely important during pregnancy. You need to be consuming at least a thousand milligrams daily. What—why are you laughing at me?"

"I'm laughing at the fact that the woman who relies on restaurants for the majority of her meals is lecturing me on the importance of calcium. Thank you for bringing all of this."

She comes over to where I'm standing and hands me a container of yogurt, "Okay. Now that we got that out of the way. Spill it. Why is David texting that you need me?"

I grab a spoon from the drawer and sit back down at the island. "He was, um, here earlier," her eyes widen and I nod, "Yeah, he was here to discuss the divorce. We discussed it and he's very willing to sign everything and just move on." My voice has taken on the same higher pitch that Lauren's did on the phone earlier. *I'm a terrible liar.*

She holds the spoon, the same spoon that she's been using to sample the ice cream, out at me like a weapon. "You're lying! Spill it now, girl. I want the details!"

I fill her in and although I try to leave out the part where we kissed, she catches on and I have to start over from the beginning. Once I finish, she takes another bite of ice cream and immediately starts trying to talk around it.

"Gah, it's cold! So, he went all caveman on you. *You wife. Never leave. Stay with David forever.* Did he drag you by your hair back to his cave?" she giggles at her own joke.

I smile. "He was very much the alpha male. I'm just glad he didn't pee on my leg to mark me as his for all eternity!"

"I'm pretty sure he did mark you, babe." She gestures to my stomach, "He just doesn't know about it yet."

I sigh and place my head in my hands on the island. "Don't remind me. This pregnancy is wreaking havoc on my emotions and my libido. He kissed me and I was all set to run away to an island with him where we could live happily ever after. It's just the pregnancy hormones—not him."

She nods sagely, "So you feel turned on like this around every male you encounter? Wait—that means when you saw Landon earlier you wanted to jump his bones!"

I make a noise of protest followed by laughter. "Lauren, no one says 'jump his bones' anymore. I think that slang went out of style like ten years ago. And to answer your question—no, I did not want to have sex with Landon when I saw him earlier. The guy still gives me the creeps and I don't fully know why."

She jumps in, "No way. A lot of people still say they want to jump someone's bones. And as far as Landon goes, you might be getting a weird vibe from him because the man is a creep. After the scene at *Nick's* that night when he grabbed you—it still gives me chills. David thinks he's the one that broke in to your house." She slaps a hand over her mouth as if that will erase what she just said.

"Lauren," my voice is very calm, "What do you mean David thinks Landon broke into the house? Have you been talking to him behind my back?"

I was almost one hundred percent certain that it was Landon, but it surprised me that David shared that suspicion as well. Back to the most pressing question of all, how does Lauren know this?

"Elizabeth, I shouldn't have said anything. Let's talk about something else. I know—how about those Rangers? I mean, they beat the White Sox last night, but boy has this season been rough. And they've got the Astros in a couple of days, it doesn't look good right now."

I push my chair back, the legs scraping loudly on the tile floor. "You're talking to David behind my back aren't you? What have you told him? Does he know I'm pregnant? Dammit, I trusted you, just like I trusted she who shall not be named. This is how you repay me?"

She comes after me as I storm out of the kitchen. "Wait! Elizabeth, wait. Just calm down!"

"Calm down? I need to calm down because yet another friend of mine has fallen under the spell that is David Greene?"

She holds her hands up and yells, "Stop shouting! It's not what you think. I swear I haven't been talking to David—his text to me tonight was the first I'd heard from him since everything happened!"

I'm practically panting with anger at this point and I push the words out through clenched teeth. "Then how do you know what David suspects in the case of the break-in? The only logical explanation is that you're talking to him."

"I'm sleeping with Mike!" She yells the words out over the last of mine and we stand in complete silence, staring at each other.

I cringe, "What? Oh my God. Laur—I'm sorry! And, congratulations? How long has this been going on? And why didn't you tell me?"

"We've been sort of dating since the night we all went out together. And I was going to tell you, but I worried about what you'd think—worried we'd end up like this."

I grab her in a rough hug, "I'm awful—I'm sorry. I'm not even going to try and blame this on pregnancy. It's just that I lost one friend already and I couldn't bear it if I lost you too."

"I know it's only been a couple of months, but I think I love him."

I grin at her through tears, "That's awesome news. He's a good guy. What did you mean by 'sort of dating' though? It seems like you're legitimately dating him if you ask me."

She moves away from me and sits down on the sofa. "Well, we didn't know how either of you would take it, so we've kept everything very low key. Anyway, I don't want to talk about it anymore. Let me see the pictures of my future niece or nephew again."

I go into the bedroom and retrieve the pictures, handing them to her as I sit down in my chair. "Laur—I know you don't wanna talk about it anymore, but seeing as to how my soon to be ex-husband left me with a severe case of female blue balls—is Mike, um, big everywhere?"

Her eyes widen, "Elizabeth Greene, you did not just ask me if my boyfriend is 'big.' Dear lord, you really are letting these hormones take over aren't you?"

I groan, "Yes. If I'm not puking, I'm dreaming up ways to seduce David. So, in light of the fact that some of us are going through a bit of dry spell, you owe me. I guess just tell me how the sex is." I sigh as though I'm exasperated before winking at her.

She leans back into the sofa, laughing. "It's a good thing I like so you much, you pervert. If you need to excuse yourself to take care of your 'situation,' I'll just play Candy Crush on my phone while I wait. Oh and to answer your question—phenomenal. It's absolutely phenomenal."

Wait, what?

"You're killing me. That's all I get? Phenomenal?"

She wipes away tears of laughter. "If I say anymore, I'm afraid you'll spontaneously combust in your chair!"

"How am I going to make it through the next thirty-one weeks of pregnancy if I'm in this constant state of arousal?"

"You'll be rubbing up against strangers on the street!" She snorts with laughter and falls apart all over again.

"You laugh now, Lauren. You won't be laughing when I move my chair over right next to you at work and hump your leg!"

"You wouldn't dare!"

It's in this moment that I realize losing Jess isn't the worst thing that could've happened. I'd clung to a friendship with someone who constantly needed the spotlight. And for a while, I was fine in the shadows. Since the accident though, I've been making my way into the light. It's nice, you know. I'm enjoying the freedom of not living in someone else's shadow and enjoying the warmth of the sun on my skin. Lauren isn't necessarily someone I would've grown close to had everything not imploded with Jess. I'm thankful for that, even though it meant losing David.

As we sit and poke fun at one another, I think that I'll be okay. I'll make it through this loss and emerge stronger. It's just impossible to imagine a future that doesn't include David.

CHAPTER ELEVEN
David

"So, David, what brings you here today?" The man sitting across from me reminds me so much of my dad that it's hard to gather my bearings at first.

I knew it was going to take more than just deciding not to drink to win Beth back, so I reached out to Dr. White. She couldn't see me due to it being a conflict of interest, with her being Beth's therapist. She did, however, refer me to Dr. Alan Gregory though.

He doesn't really resemble my old man, but there's something about him that just makes me feel like opening up. He's probably in his mid-sixties with long, graying hair that he has tied back in a ponytail. He's wearing jeans and a Polo—not quite what I expected, but considering I'm as blue collar as they come, I appreciate the fact that he's not in a suit. I think that was my biggest fear in coming here, feeling like I might not be able to open up and be myself.

Dr. Gregory—or Alan, as he's asked me to call him—asked for me to plan on being here for about two hours, with it being our first visit. I'm glad as I spend the entire first hour recounting the events that led me here.

I told myself I wouldn't bring up my dad, yet it's the first thing out of my mouth. I'm pouring my guts out to a relative stranger and in a weird way, it feels so good to get it off my chest.

He just listens intently to me and encourages me to continue when I get quiet.

"D—Alan, I'm telling you things I never even told my wife. That's a little unnerving, you know?"

He chuckled, "David, sometimes it's easier to talk about the difficult things in a setting like this. There's no fear of reproach or condemnation. You have the floor during our time together. I will offer my thoughts when necessary, but right now you're getting your story out in the open. In order for me to best help you, you have to tell me your story in your own words. From there, we can sift through it and extract key pieces."

I leave his office feeling lighter than I have since I lost my old man. I'm scheduled to meet with him again in a week. *No wonder Beth wanted to go to Dr. White.* She was probably able to finally open up about all the negative surrounding us.

I pick up my phone and tap her name in. I look over at the clock in my truck and see that it's almost noon. She gets off work early on Fridays and I need to see her. It's been over a week. I also don't have anywhere to be this afternoon as my foreman assured me everything was under control on our current job site.

Me:

Good afternoon, baby.

Can I pick you up for lunch?

Beth:

Baby? Are you day drinking now?

Did you forget we're getting a divorce?

Me:

Like I told you the other night, I've got sixty days.

FORSAKING ALL OTHERS

And if I remember correctly, you seemed to be having second thoughts as well.

Beth:
David—I can't. It'll just make it harder.

Me:
Funny, you did that the other night too!
Seriously, just let me take you to lunch—one lunch, Beth.

Beth:
Fine. One lunch, but this doesn't change anything.

That's where you're wrong, baby. It changes everything.

I pull up and park in her office parking lot. I find that twisting my wedding band in circles around my finger is a good distraction. Alan didn't say anything in regards to my contact with Beth, but I need this to go well. I need for her to see how good we are together and I'm under a tremendous amount of stress out of this fear that I'll screw it up.

The side door of the office building opens up and out walks Beth. She's wearing a long black tank top over white capris and her hair is again pulled up in her signature messy bun. The sun glares off of her glasses and she raises a hand in an attempt to shield them. I can't take my eyes off of her. She scans the lot before she sees my truck. I can't help it, I'm fucking giddy when I see the smile on her face.

I get out and go around to open the passenger door for her. I end up wrapping my hands around her hips, lifting her up into the truck as she looks up at me with a smirk.

"I was promised lunch with no strings attached. Might you know anything about this?"

I settle her into her seat and press my lips to hers before answering, "Yep, just lunch between friends—no expectations."

Her eyes darken and her lips part slightly, "Just lunch," she repeats before snapping out of her stupor and continuing, "I'm starving—where are we headed?"

I drive us to a little café that we used to frequent when we were first married. I watch her face for signs of recognition and I'm a little disappointed when there are none. I know she's still regaining her memory and the doctor said it would take some time, but damn do I wish she could remember us—and not just the bad parts.

"Where are we?"

I clear my throat, "Just a little place I think you'll like."

We head inside, out of the blazing heat, and over to an empty booth tucked into the corner. The red leather is worn and the entire place could probably use a good updating—in my head, I decide which walls I would tear down. I think these are the original booths from the late sixties, but they serve the best chicken fried steak around so I can overlook the décor.

A television is on in the corner, broadcasting the local news to the handful of people joining us in the café.

Beth sits down across from me, seemingly lost in thought, so it surprises the hell out of her when I reach across the table for her hand.

She gives me a warning look, but doesn't pull away. It's yet another confirmation in my mind that we can come back from this. I run my thumb along her wrist, enjoying the feel of her soft skin against my callused fingers.

Our waitress comes up to get our drink orders. She looks every bit the café waitress. Her gray hair is up in a tight bun, a pencil tucked behind one ear. Her old-school black glasses sit perched on her nose as she holds her notepad in one hand. "What can I get you two lovebirds?"

Beth pulls her hand away and I'm about to protest when I see her eyes are glued to the television set. The news anchors are showing a picture of a woman that I don't recognize, but Beth sure seems to know who she is. She stands up and moves closer and I order two waters before following her.

"We are bringing you the case of a missing person this afternoon. Katya Egorichev, age thirty-two, was last seen on August 7th. She is 5'11" and has brown hair and green eyes. Egorichev, originally from Colorado, was in the area visiting friends when she disappeared. Her car was found at the hotel she had been staying at, along with her cell phone and personal belongings. If you have any information on the whereabouts of Katya Egorichev, you are urged to call the Crimestoppers hotline at—"

I tune out the rest and focus on Beth. She looks like she's seen a ghost and nearly jumps out of her skin when I touch her.

"Beth, who is she? Do you know her?"

Her voice is barely above a whisper, "It's Katya—Landon's ex-girlfriend. He told me they broke up—back before the accident. I ran into him last Thursday."

My blood runs cold. I knew he was shady, but this is putting him into a whole other category. This is Ted Bundy crazy—I just wonder if the police department is aware he's the man they need to focus in on. I'm just thinking I need to call Mike when I see Beth's face has drained of all color.

"I'm not feeling very well, David." I place my arm around her in an attempt to get her back to the booth when she goes limp in my arms. I sink down to the floor with her, never letting go.

"Help me!" I call out to the waitress as I cradle my wife's limp body in my arms. *She fainted—literally passed the fuck out from seeing that.*

"Beth? Open your eyes, baby."

The waitress, Deb, comes back over with a wet towel and a glass of water.

I place the towel on her face, hoping it will jar her back to consciousness and I'm instantly rewarded with the sight of those big baby blues.

She blinks a few times before she realizes she's lying on the restaurant floor.

"What happened?"

"You fainted after seeing the news story on that missing girl. How do you feel now?"

She closes her eyes again and I worry she's fainted again on me when she finally speaks. "Truthfully? I feel pretty damn embarrassed. Any chance that everyone in the restaurant left and no one saw?" Her eyes open again and fixate on me.

Another customer chooses that moment to interrupt. "Do you need me to call an ambulance? Is she going to be okay?"

I nod at the man, "She's going to be fine. Her blood sugar got a little low and left her lightheaded. Thank you for your concern though."

She smiles at me as he walks off, "Thanks. Any chance we can get our food to go?"

CHAPTER
TWELVE
Beth

I'm giving myself a headache in an effort to make sense of everything. I remember just enough about Landon to be concerned, but not enough to provide myself with any concrete evidence. I have this sick feeling in the pit of my stomach that actually has nothing to do with morning sickness. At least, I don't think so—the fainting thing might be related to the pregnancy though.

David ordered us a couple of plates to go while I sat with my head down in the booth. My cheeks burned with embarrassment at drawing the entire café's attention. We managed to make it home where he promptly ordered me into bed. I can hear him banging away in the kitchen as he gets our lunch ready; I've got the strangest feeling of déjà vu, but it's comforting.

"Hey Beth? Do we still have those wooden T.V. trays?"

"Check the pantry. They're on one of the lower shelves in the back." *What?* Seriously? I cannot remember whether or not Landon is a good person, but I can sure tell you where the T.V. trays are kept.

David comes back in a few minutes later with a tray. He gently sets it in front of me before going back to grab his food. I look at my plate—the chicken fried steak is cut into bite-sized pieces. It's such a simple gesture, but this man is killing me. Just when I think I've got it figured out, he shows up and turns everything upside down.

I blink rapidly and fan my eyes—*do not cry...do not cry...*

"Baby, you okay?"

I look up at him, although my vision is slightly distorted from the unshed tears. "I'm fine. Just tired."

He eyes me warily before climbing into bed. We eat in silence while my brain swirls violently back and forth between the man beside me and the man who may or may not be responsible for Katya's disappearance. *Maybe the divorce is a mistake... Could Landon truly be capable of violence?* My eyelids grow heavy, something I'm experiencing a lot more with the pregnancy and I drift off.

I awaken hours later to a tickling sensation on my cheek. I'm lying on my side and David's body is spooned around mine, his nose buried in my hair and his beard tickling my face. His arm is draped across my hip and his hand absentmindedly strokes my stomach. I still.

Does he know?

"Does Jess know you're here right now?" I don't know why I say it. It's unfair, but I could easily slip into this role of playing house with him if I'm not careful. I'm wrapped up in a dangerous fantasy here.

His hand stops moving and I can feel him stiffen up behind me. His voice sounds gravelly when he finally answers me. "No, she doesn't know I'm here. Why? —you call up Landon and let him know?"

I exhale forcefully, my bladder giving me a painful reminder to end this argument before it gets out of hand, "No—I haven't spoken to Landon since that day in the parking lot. Considering his ex-girlfriend is missing, I doubt he'd care."

"You think he did it?"

His question surprises me and I roll over to face him, my unruly hair falling in waves over my face. I brush it out of my eyes and whisper, "I don't know. I'm sure he's suspect number one though."

He reaches out and tucks more strands of hair behind my ear, "I'm not comfortable leaving you alone until we have more answers."

I pull away from him, "You can't make that call, David," I sit up in bed and gesture at him, "You—being here—it's confusing as hell. I want you almost as much as I want my next breath, but you're having a baby with Jess. I can't foresee any outcome that works for us."

He sits up and grabs onto my arms, "So, you want me. You don't want to be with Landon?"

My head drops in frustration, "That's what you took away from this? No, I don't want Landon. I can't relate to the woman that cheated on her husband. It makes me sick, but it doesn't change the fact that it happened," I pull away and swing my legs down off of the bed, "Now, I have to pee so can we put this on hold for a sec?"

"Yep." He comes around to help me up.

"I'm fine."

"Beth, you passed out earlier. I'm not taking any more chances with you today."

He guides me into the bathroom, but doesn't leave. "Uh, David, could you wait outside?"

He grumbles about having seen it all before, but leaves nonetheless.

It's afterward, when I'm washing my hands that the nausea decides to make a sudden reappearance. I clench my teeth together in a vain attempt to keep the chicken fried steak in my stomach. I will force my stomach to obey me.

Just wait until he's gone.

Once he's gone, I can vomit to my heart's content. Seriously?

Please stomach, I'll give you a cracker.

My stomach and I are not on the same page. I begin dry heaving and then my lunch comes up, followed by breakfast. I'm trying to do it as quietly as possible, but I hear the bathroom door open.

"Beth? Jesus, are you okay?" David comes over and pulls my hair back out of my face, "Let me get you a wet washcloth."

I nod, or at least I think I do and sit back against the wall. He places the cold washcloth against the back of my neck and picks me up as though I weigh nothing. After letting me brush my teeth, he lifts me again. A small part of me thinks I should fight him on this, but I don't have the energy at the moment. He talks to me as he carries me back to bed, the deep timbre of his voice soothes me.

"—you ate the same thing as me so I wonder if you might have a bug or maybe just the stress of the day got to you." He places me on the bed before continuing his thoughts, "Either way, I want you in bed resting. I'll run out and get you some ginger ale—"

I place my hand on his arm, "David, you've done enough. Really. I just need to sleep and I'll feel better. You can go, I'll be fine."

He tenses up, "I already told you I'm not leaving you alone. Not until we know for sure that Landon had nothing to do with that girl's disappearance. Why do you have to be so stubborn?"

I push him away and lay my head back on the pillow, "Why'd

you have to sleep with my best friend?"

He reels back as though I've slapped him. It's low, but I'm scared he'll find out I'm more than just sick if he stays here any longer. I can't handle the added stress right now.

His voice is quiet, "I'm going to go out and get you a few things. I'll be back later." He skips over the emotional slap I just gave him and kisses me on the cheek before leaving.

I'm an asshole.

I grab my phone off of the nightstand, nearly upending a glass of water in the process. I send a text to Lauren.

Me:

You free tonight? I'm thinking the only way I'm going to get David out of this house is if you sleep over.

Lauren:

I don't have plans, but wouldn't you rather David sleep over? I'll just run you a nice cold shower if you get all hot and bothered again.

Me:

**Had my head in the toilet about twenty minutes ago...
not really in the mood for romance.
See if Mike can take David out and then we'll be golden.**

Lauren:

There's a missing person case he's been working on, so I haven't had a chance to see him today. I doubt he'll be leaving the office anytime soon though.

SHANNON MYERS

Me:

Yeah, I heard about that.

We can discuss it more when you get here.

Lauren:

Let me finish up this load of laundry

and I'll head your way in an hour or so.

I place the phone back on the nightstand along with my glasses. I'll just rest my eyes for a few minutes.

I'm at a large indoor pool, swimming laps, when I hear an infant cry. I stop swimming and begin looking around. There's a baby no more than a few hours old lying on one of those inflatable rafts in the middle of the pool. Its screams echo off the concrete walls and I begin to swim toward it as fast as I can. Somehow the pool has gotten larger and it seems to be taking me forever to get there. I feel its wailing in every fiber of my being and I know that this isn't some random child—it's my baby. I urge my body to move faster, my heart racing. I'm about ten feet away when the raft begins to disintegrate and the child slips into the water. The cries stop immediately and I scream "no" until my voice is hoarse. I dive under the water and reach out my arms for it. Just as I'm about to make contact, strong arms wrap around me and pull me back toward the surface. I'm fighting for all I'm worth now to get free, but it's useless. The person holding me is too strong.

"Hush, you're safe now. You're safe now." Landon's words chill me and I continue struggling in his arms.

"My baby! My baby! Let me go!" I can see the baby still struggling and anguish covers me like a blanket.

He's got this maniacal grin on his face and he grips me even tighter, "You're safe here. Shhhh.....Shhhh...You're safe here."

"Shhhh...Beth, you're safe. Wake up!"

I sit up with a scream, wrapped in strong arms. I begin fighting to break free, convinced Landon is still holding on to me.

"Beth, baby, it's me! Stop fighting me."

I begin weeping. Guttural sobs wrack my body. *What the fuck was that?* It felt so real.

David pulls me into him, rocking us back and forth on the bed. He doesn't ask any questions and I briefly wonder if nightmares are a common occurrence with me. I'm an out-of-control hormonal wreck, bouncing between emotions like a pinball machine, and yet here he is. Holding me. Loving me.

His hands tangle in my hair as he crushes me to his chest. My heart is still pounding and I try to steady my breathing.

He murmurs into my hair, "Good girl. Deep breaths—in and out. I've got you. I'm not letting you go."

I cling to him, "It was a nightmare, but it felt like it was real."

He laughs, "You were screaming the house down when I walked in," his laugh dies away, "I thought someone was hurting you. I ran in here ready to fight and you were thrashing around screaming about a baby."

I stop breathing. *No.*

I try to make my voice sound calm, "Oh?"

He doesn't seem to notice my reaction and continues, "Yeah. I didn't understand at first, but I think I do now."

Here we go.

He elaborates, "You've had to deal with the fact that I'm having a baby with someone else and you wish it was us. I get it. If I could go back and do things differently, I would. The fact that it's causing you nightmares kills me."

I exhale slowly, "I guess I didn't look at it that way."

I'm safe. My secret will remain just that. I'm feeling pretty proud of myself for not giving anything away, so much so that I don't think through my next actions.

I pull back slightly and look up at him. The last remaining rays of sunlight filter through the window, illuminating his face. His hair and beard look almost golden brown in the light, he's absolutely stunning. I press my lips to his jaw, my eyes never leaving his. I kiss a trail down his jawline and stop at the corner of his mouth. He's remaining absolutely still, but I can feel his heart beating out a strong rhythm underneath my hand.

I close my eyes and move my mouth over his. For a man whose hands are callused and rough from years of hard labor, his lips are surprisingly soft. The sparks are off the charts and I worry that they'll light a fuse, causing me to self-destruct. I ignore my doubts and instead turn reason over to my mouth, exploring the man I pledged to love until death.

He lays me against the pillows and my hands move down to grip the hem of his t-shirt. He grabs the back of the collar and lifts it over his head effortlessly, his ink on full display. Tattoos coat his muscular arms, the corded veins a testament to how hard he's worked to get his company where it is today. *He's never been afraid to get his hands dirty.* I pause as the memory catches me off guard. Memories of him coming in from work—early in our marriage, covered in sawdust and drywall, pour in and I remember vividly that he never once complained about how hard it was to get his company launched.

"You want a notebook for all the studying you're doing over there?"

I look up at his face, "I can't help it. I didn't exactly get a lot of time to look you over the last time."

He smiles and leans down, lifting my tank top up and over my head, "My turn...I didn't get to see you the last time."

I giggle, "Liar."

He brings his mouth back down over mine and my only thought is *more*. More of this. More of him. I don't think it'll ever be enough, which is going to make this even more difficult. I'm letting him in on an impulse, but I fear that when he leaves he'll be taking a big part of me with him.

He rocks his body into mine and I arch up into him, needing the friction. A moan involuntarily escapes and he takes it as his cue to continue. David uses one hand to brace himself, while the other is on my lower back, guiding me. He can't be comfortable in those jeans, but he doesn't seem to be in any hurry to get them off. I reach down and fumble my way through undoing his belt buckle while his hand moves up to unclasp my bra. I free him from his jeans and boxer briefs and pull him into me. *I'm so close.* My breathing becomes heavier and he increases his movements against me. I come with a cry and a death grip on his waist. *Does pregnancy make orgasms more intense?*

He stops moving against me, "Watching you come is absolutely fucking beautiful, babe."

My breathing is ragged and I can't find my voice. I unbutton my Capri pants, but his hand stops me.

"No. We're not doing that."

I scoff, "Why the hell not?"

"I told you I was going to win you back. Until you call off the divorce, this is as far as it goes."

I sit up and reach for my bra, "You're serious right now? You're going to hold out unless I call off the divorce? Who does that?"

He adjusts himself as he pulls his pants back up. Seeing as to how he's still rock hard, I'm not sure how he's expecting that to work. "I'm serious, Beth. I want you forever, not one night. I think you'll find that I can be very patient."

He reaches for his shirt just as we hear a voice call out from the living room, "You know who else is patient? Me. I've been sitting here quietly playing Candy Crush for the last twenty minutes while you two are in there not having sex."

I stifle a laugh and look over to see David is grinning as well. *Leave it to Lauren to lighten the mood.* He tosses me my shirt and I try and make myself look presentable before leaving our bedroom.

We exit the room sheepishly, like a couple of teenagers just busted for breaking curfew. Lauren is sitting on the couch with her feet propped up on the ottoman, happily playing on her phone.

She glances up at us. "Well, hey there! I made myself comfortable. I hope that's okay. What am I saying? Of course it is. I probably could've loaded up the nice electronics without anyone noticing," She tosses her phone down on the couch, "Now, who needs a cold shower?"

CHAPTER THIRTEEN
David

I laugh at Lauren's words, but I am in desperate need of a cold shower or at the very least, non-restrictive clothing.

"Lauren, you staying the night?"

She grins, "Yes, under one condition."

I gesture for her to spit it out, "And that condition would be?"

"Promise me that you eased her sexual tension and that I don't have to be worried about her sneaking into my room tonight."

I look over at Beth, her face turning a lovely shade of crimson. Forgetting the physical discomfort I'm in for a moment, I give her a seductive smile, "I dunno, baby. You gonna be good for a while or should we go back and try again?"

She refuses to make eye contact with me when she answers, her eyes glued to the carpet. "Nope, I'm good. Thanks for lunch earlier."

I walk over and stand in front of her until she looks up. I lower my voice, "You sure?"

Before she can answer, I pull her into me, my mouth claiming hers as mine. I pull away when she puts her hands on my chest. "Let me know if you change your mind, Beth," I glance at Lauren on my way to the door, "Lauren, always a pleasure."

She looks up from the phone she seems to have picked up again, "Same here, David. Same here. Oh, call Mike when you get a chance. I was supposed to tell you the minute I got here, but I decided that was a sight I did not need ingrained in my mind," she waves cheerily, "Take care."

I towel dry off after a long, somewhat satisfying shower and fish a pair of black sweatpants out of my bag. I should probably unpack my things and put them into drawers, but I feel like that would make this seem like a permanent thing.

No, I've just got to keep doing what I'm doing. If I can just keep her wanting more, she might be more receptive to the idea of us working things out. I just found release in the shower, the thought of her beautiful face at the forefront of my mind, and here I am getting hard just thinking about being back in the same house as her.

The clock says it's just after eleven, but I know Mike will still be up.

"Hey man, did you just get my message?"

I laugh, "Not exactly. Your girlfriend was trying not to interrupt. What's going on?"

He sighs heavily, "I tried to call you earlier. I'm not sure if you've seen the news or not, but there's a missing person case involving someone who was intimate with Landon Scott. He voluntarily came in for questioning and to be honest with you, the guy's a wreck. He's been nothing, but forthcoming with any information he has—"

I interrupt him, "So, you're calling to tell me what exactly, Mike? That you still don't have anything on him?"

"Well, partly. The main reason I'm calling is because his alibi for August seventh involves Elizabeth. David, I've got to bring her in for an interview. I wanted to give you a head's up before that happened though."

I rub at my temple in frustration. *Shit.*

"You might as well bring me in too, man. I saw them together that day."

The line is silent for a minute, "Yeah, why don't you both come in tomorrow morning. I'll be up here for a while, but I may run home and try to get a couple of hours of sleep. Could we meet at nine?"

I agree and hang up. I can't see how corroborating that Beth was with Landon for all of twenty minutes will make much of a difference, but what do I know? I can't say that I'm not a little pleased that he's on their radar. He's going to go down for her disappearance—how could he not?

Beth was addicted to those true crime shows on television and Friday nights were spent watching *Dateline* or *20/20*. It seemed like every case involved the spouse or significant other, no matter what the crime scene seemed to suggest.

My phone buzzes in my pocket and I pull it out to see Jess's name flash across the screen. I'm tempted to hit *decline*, but I've avoided her calls for the last couple of days. I've got to be a man and face the fact that I'm going to be a parent—even if it is with the wrong woman. Although I've still got hope that the paternity test will let me off the hook.

"Hello?"

"David—you do know how to answer your phone. I've been trying to reach you for the past few days."

"Yeah, I know. I didn't have much to say. Figured we'd talk once the test results come back. Did you make the appointment with the lab?"

Her voice breaks, "I need to see you. Can I come over?"

I shake my head, "Are you serious? It's almost midnight, Jess. No, you can't come over. There's nothing we need to talk about now that can't wait until morning."

"I want to show you the pictures from the visit. You ran out of there and missed the ultrasound."

I massage my temple again, this time with more force, "No. I can't tonight—"

She talks over me, "We need to talk about living arrangements once the baby comes. Do you think Lizzie will move out of the house? I think we'd have more room there than at my place—"

"Do not say her name. I don't want you approaching her about this shit either. We are not going to live together, Jess. You wanna know why? Because we're not a family—there is no scenario where we end up together and raise this baby. I'm married to Beth and that's not going to change."

She laughs bitterly, "Married? For how much longer, David? I know that she filed for divorce. Hell, half the town probably knows it by now. You might want to consider that there's only one person still willing to have a life with you, and that's me."

Should I be the asshole now or wait and let her get a few more digs in first?

Now is as good a time as any.

"Jess, not like it's any of your business, but Beth and I have been spending more time together. I actually just got back from the house," I can hear her crying, "If the tests show that this kid is mine, I'll share custody with you. Until—"

She raises her voice, "David, stop! I've loved you since that night at *Nick's* when you met Lizzie. I knew we had something special...I just married the wrong guy!"

FORSAKING ALL OTHERS

I stop pacing and sit down on the edge of the bed. I pinch the bridge of my nose, the headache growing worse by the second. "Jess, please stop talking. You're embarrassing yourself. Even if Beth and I can't make things work, you and I will never be together. What happened between us is fucked up at best, definitely not a good foundation to build a relationship on. I'll parent with you, but that's all it will ever be. You never answered me before. Did your doctor's office get you an appointment for the test?"

Jess sniffs into the phone, "Yeah. They couldn't get us in until September eighth at ten," she laughs humorlessly, "I guess there's a lot of people around this town who are unsure of who knocked them up."

Jesus—three weeks? I was hoping it'd be done within a few days. In three weeks, I expected to have an answer. I get the location for the lab and get the hell off of the phone.

I shut off the lights and beg sleep to come easily.

The next morning, I stop and grab a couple of coffees on the way to my house. I called Beth first thing this morning and let her know that we were needed at the police station. She didn't seem surprised by the revelation, but then again she watches enough television to expect this sort of thing to happen.

Lauren's car is gone when I pull up and park. I walk across the damp grass and balance the coffees in one hand while ringing the doorbell with the other. Our next door neighbor, Charles, is out in his front yard messing around the flower bed. He waves and then gives me a questioning look. He's in his late sixties and prides himself on being the neighborhood watch program. Seriously, I doubt anyone else needs to participate as he seems to know everything that's going on at all times.

I smile and return the wave, "Hey Chuck—left my garage door opener so I'm locked out." He hates when I call him Chuck, so I make it a point to do it often.

He nods, but still keeps his eyes on me.

Nosy bastard.

Beth opens the door and I see that she's dressed up for the occasion. She's wearing dark wash jeans with a grey t-shirt and black blazer. Her hair is down and somewhat tame today. I swear, those blonde curls are my kryptonite.

"Hey. I'm just going to grab my shoes and we can go."

She runs back into the bedroom and I set her coffee down on the kitchen counter while I wait.

I grab my cup and sip the hot liquid, trying to force my exhausted brain to function. I tossed and turned all night with thoughts of Jess, Beth, and even Landon. Needless to say, I'll be looking forward to a Saturday afternoon nap.

Beth comes into the kitchen and immediately wrinkles her nose. "What is that smell? It smells like something is burning."

She sniffs the air and I hold up her coffee. "I got you coffee. Is that what you're smelling?"

She looks at the cup like it contains poison and begins gagging. I'm still trying to process what the hell is wrong with her when she calmly walks over to the sink and vomits.

Her voice sounds strangled, "Please get rid of it. Throw it in the dumpster—whatever, just get it out of this house."

I walk out to the alley and throw the coffee in the dumpster, but not before noting that the lawn needs to be mowed. I'll take care of that after we get back from the station.

FORSAKING ALL OTHERS

Beth is standing by the garage door, drinking water as though nothing is wrong.

"Are you still sick from yesterday?"

She swallows and nods, "Yeah, it must be like a twenty-four hour bug or something. I hope you don't get it."

We ride to the police station in silence. I sip my coffee while she flips through the radio stations like most men (myself included) do with the T.V. remote. She finally settles on some god-awful pop radio station and hums quietly to herself.

I take another sip of coffee and she rolls down the window, looking a little pale. "Beth, you okay? Feeling sick again?"

She is turned so that the wind is blowing right into her face and I see her nod. I pull the car as far over onto the shoulder of the highway as I can and she stumbles out, vomiting into the grass and wildflowers growing on the side of the road. I slide across the seats and hold her hair back so she doesn't get sick on herself.

Beth wipes the back of her hand across her mouth when she finishes and I help her back into the truck. She closes her eyes and leans her head back against the seat.

"Hopefully, this will be quick and I can get you home into bed. Maybe you just need to sleep it off."

She nods again and I notice her teeth are clenched together. I pop open the console and fish around until I find a peppermint. "Try this, they're good for nausea."

"Thank you," she whispers before unwrapping it and popping it into her mouth.

We manage to make it to the police station downtown without having to pull over again. Beth seems to be feeling much better once she gets out the truck, but I hand her a few more peppermints just in case.

"How many of these do you have?"

I laugh at her question, "Well, I eat at *Sonic* a lot so I've probably got a whole console full of them."

She places her hand on my arm, "You eat out every day? That's really bad, David. You need to take better care of yourself."

Her words touch me. Regardless of what's going on between us, she still feels something for me. I grab her hand as we walk across the street, "That's what I've got you for, Beth. Make sure I'm eating right, getting eight hours of sleep—you know, important things like that."

She laughs, "And here I thought you were just using me for sex." I smile and grip her hand tighter. She doesn't pull away from me so we walk hand in hand into the station.

There's just enough moisture in the air for it to feel slightly humid, a rarity in west Texas, and I can already tell it's going to be unbearably hot later. I just hope we can get in and out so that I can mow without feeling like I'm standing on the surface of the sun.

They take us to different rooms to interview us separately, something I did not plan on happening. Mike assures me that this is normal procedure as he walks me to an interview room.

"So, you never told me how you came to be an alibi witness. Care to elaborate?"

I shrug my shoulders, "I was sitting in a parking lot and saw her come out of her doctor's appointment. I was across the street so I had a pretty clear view of her. Landon came up out of nowhere and they talked for about twenty minutes. Nothing to elaborate really—it's not like I heard what they were saying."

Mike stops walking and turns around to face me, "Did Elizabeth know you were there?"

I roll my eyes, "No, she didn't know I was there. I mean, I told her about it later."

He runs his hand through his hair, "Jesus Christ, David. You're camped out in a parking lot just waiting for her to leave an appointment?"

I stiffen, "Mike—Landon came up out of nowhere. Obviously, he was watching her. Thank God I was there to make sure she was safe!"

"How is what you were doing any different than what he was doing? You were stalking your wife, man! That doesn't make you look any better than him at this point."

"Now you sound like Beth. I was at Jess's appointment with her. We had words and I left. I was taking care of a few things with work when she walked out. She looked a bit unnerved so I was making sure she got to her car when he walked up. And, really? Can one really stalk their own wife? I think that's called being a good husband. You happy now, detective? Is this part of my interview?"

He reaches out and puts his hand on my shoulder. "Calm down, this isn't part of the interview. It's just your best friend worrying about you. I want it to work out between you two, more than anything, but I also want you to remain rooted in reality. Don't kill yourself chasing after a woman who doesn't want to be caught."

I give him a curt nod, seething on the inside. It's getting really old, hearing advice from people who have no idea what's going on between me and my wife.

"Alright, Dear Abby, let's get this shit over with."

CHAPTER FOURTEEN
Beth

I sit on a hard plastic chair, resting my arms on the table in front of me in an otherwise empty room. There's a one-way mirror along the wall in front of me and I can't help but feel nervous. I have to remind myself that I'm not a suspect in Katya's disappearance—something that's easy to forget when sitting here.

At least I don't feel like barfing anymore. I used to love coffee, but for the last few weeks the smell of it sends me running for a toilet. I really hope David still thinks I have a bug and isn't starting to suspect anything else.

Mike walks into the room with a man and woman I don't recognize.

"Elizabeth, this is Carole Shaffer—she's representing Landon Scott and this is Adam Perry—he's a special investigator that will be interviewing you today."

I nod at both of them, "Nice to meet you."

Adam sits down across from me, "Do you have any questions before we begin?"

"No, I don't think so." I try to calm my shaking hands in my lap.

He continues, "Mrs. Greene, just so you're aware, this interview is being recorded. Have you ever been interviewed in this capacity before?"

I let him know that I haven't.

FORSAKING ALL OTHERS

"Are you aware of why you're being interviewed this morning?"

"Yes, it's regarding the disappearance of Katya Egorichev and my interaction with Landon Scott."

"How familiar are you with this case?"

I shrug, "Not very, I saw it on the news yesterday. I know she's been missing for over a week. I also know that she was dating Landon Scott, but I believe that relationship ended back in May."

Landon's lawyer scribbles something on a piece of paper, but otherwise remains silent.

The rest of the questions consist of where I was last Thursday. I recount my day from the time I woke up until running into Landon. The investigator asks a lot of questions about that interaction and I answer everything as best I can.

Afterward, I'm ready for lunch and a nap. I've found that if I wait too long to eat it makes the nausea even worse. I pop another peppermint into my mouth as I sit on a bench outside, waiting for David to finish his interview.

Just as I'm about to text him, he comes storming out of the building, the glass doors rattling behind him.

"Let's go." His voice is cold and I have to jog to keep up with him.

"What happened in there?" I'm panting slightly, but I'm going to blame that on the pregnancy and not the fact that I haven't stepped foot inside a gym in the last two months.

He unlocks the truck and walks around to the passenger side to help me in, "Nothing. Just got a lot of shit to get done today—don't wanna waste another second here."

We drive back to the house in complete silence, even the radio is turned off. Even without my full memory I can tell he's furious, the anger radiates from him. I just wish I knew why he was so upset. I think back to when we got to the station and he seemed fine. I mean, we were holding hands so surely it's not anything I've done.

He parks in the driveway when we get back and helps me out before going into the garage. The broody silent treatment isn't working for me so I follow him.

"You wanna tell me what happened back there? You were fine when we got there, but now you're obviously upset. I just want to know why."

He pulls the lawnmower out from the back corner of the garage and begins checking the gas and oil levels. "I'm fine. I told you—I have a lot to accomplish today. Go on inside and get some lunch."

I sigh, but my rumbling stomach begs me to take his advice. I make a turkey sandwich and eat it as I make him one as well. This is getting complicated. I'm not sure how I thought that I could file for divorce and keep emotion out of it, but I did. Now, I've got a brooding alpha outside mowing and I'm worrying about why he's upset, while fixing him lunch.

To make matters worse, I find myself dreaming about the next time he'll kiss me. *We're acting like we did when we were dating.* I laugh at the thought. We were constantly making out, but not having sex. I didn't realize I'd be back in the same boat five years later. I've crossed a line and there's no way I'm walking away unscathed at this point. I don't want to keep pushing him away, but I'm not okay with playing stepmom to Jess's baby. I'd constantly be worried that she was trying to stick her claws into him again. Maybe I just enjoy these next few weeks and then tell him goodbye.

I hear the lawnmower stop and decide it's a good time to

interrupt. I carry the plate of food and a glass of iced tea out into the garage, but I don't see David anywhere. The front yard is finished so I walk through the gate into the backyard. He's crouched down over the lawnmower with a wrench in his hand, doing God knows what, but looking good while doing it. The muscles in his forearms stand out as he tightens something.

"I brought you some lunch." It's comes out sounding raspy as my mouth has suddenly gone dry.

"Thanks." He doesn't even turn around.

I place everything on the patio table and wait for him to come over. He stands up and there's a mixture of grease and oil on his hands and shirt. He goes over and turns on the faucet on the outdoor sink, scrubbing up with soap and a brush, and I'm so mesmerized by his rugged hands that I don't initially notice that he won't make eye contact with me.

What would have happened that he can't even bear to look at me?

The truth hits me like a sucker punch.

Landon.

It's the only thing that makes sense. Being at the police station was a stark reminder that my hands are just as dirty as his in this whole situation.

"I'm sorry, David. I'm so sorry for all of this." My voice is so quiet that I'm not sure he hears me at first until I see him stiffen up.

I continue, "I knew it would come to this, a time when you couldn't even look at me without seeing what I've done to you. If I could change the past, I would. I would do it in a heartbeat."

I turn to go back inside when I hear the water shut off and suddenly he's right in front of me. He picks me up and backs me up against the bricks, my legs locking instinctively behind him. I look up at him in surprise, "Dav—"

His mouth covers mine, effectively silencing my words. I'm sure I've got grease stains on my clothes, but I couldn't care less right now.

When he pulls back, his fierce blue eyes pin me with their gaze, "Never you. Do you hear me? There will never be a point that I won't want you. You don't owe me an apology. Mike just said some stuff at the station earlier—got in my head. He told me to quit chasing after someone who didn't want to be caught."

I inhale sharply, "He thinks you're wasting your time?"

He tightens his grip on me before answering, "Yeah. It got me thinking that maybe I'm coming on too strong with you. I told you I was going to win you back and I intend to keep that promise, but I need to know that you want this too. Even if it's just a small part of you."

I don't hesitate, "I want this too." Damn the repercussions.

Surprise flashes in his eyes for a moment and then it's gone and he reclaims my mouth.

I pull back, breathing hard. "Does this mean we can have sex now?" I'm pressed right up against his jeans and based on what I'm feeling, I'm hoping his answer is a resounding yes.

He laughs and shakes his head, "No. I wanna take this slow. There's no need to rush anything."

I close my eyes and groan, "You're killing me over here."

He leans down until his forehead rests against mine. "I said we're not having sex. I never said I wouldn't keep you satisfied."

My eyes fly wide open, "Oh really?" I chuckle, "You're using the phrase I gave you when we were dating against me now? I'm surprised you remembered."

He shifts me in his arms, "Well, I'm more surprised that you remember. It does feel like starting over though, yeah?"

I nod, relishing in the heat of the sun and the feel of his arms around me. I could stop time right now and be perfectly content. My mind has other plans though. There are things I haven't asked him, questions I wasn't sure I wanted the answer to. I feel like if we're going to attempt to make this work, I need to know.

I break the silence, "Do you think it's your baby?"

His jaw tightens, "No, I don't."

I swallow the lump in my throat, "How…um…I mean, do you know…" I trail off, unsure of how to ask the question.

"Just spit it out, Beth." He sounds so defeated in this moment that I wish I could take back the words. I don't want to cause a bigger rift between us, but I need to know.

"How many times were you and her…together?"

He gently sets me back on my feet and takes a step back, "We're doing this right now?" He sighs, "Okay. I slept with her three times. Your turn. How many times were you with him?"

Suddenly the heat isn't as welcoming as I previously thought. I turn, without a word, and walk inside. He follows me.

"That's not fair, Beth. You asked me a question that I truthfully answered. I deserve the same from you."

I take a deep breath and turn around, "I don't know, David. I don't know how many times Landon and I slept together. A lot of it is still a blur. You happy now?"

He nods through clenched teeth, looking anything but happy.

I soften my voice, "You slept with her after your dad died. When were the other two times?"

"You're sure we have to have this conversation right now?" He sits down on the arm of the couch, the same place he was sitting the night I found out about the affair. The irony is not lost on me.

"I just want to know as much as I can so we can figure out how to move forward. I don't want to run into her again and not know. The last time was bad enough."

He holds his hand up, 'Wait, what happened the last time you saw her?"

"She confronted me over the whole thing, wanted me to know that she never meant to hurt me. Shit you say to someone when you eat the last bar of chocolate—not what you to say to someone after you've slept with their husband." I huff in frustration and he laughs at me. I've missed that laugh.

"Last bar of chocolate? Girls apologize to each other for that stuff?"

I nod my head in mock seriousness, "Absolutely. Chocolate is very important to us. Now, quit stalling."

He runs his hand through his beard, as though he's trying to decide where to start. "I—shit, Beth—I'm an asshole. Okay? What I did...to you...to us..." He trails off and I go over to him, kneeling down between his legs.

"You think what I did helped our relationship? I'm just as guilty as you are in this, so stop treating me with kid gloves." I rest my arms on his muscular thighs and wait for him to continue.

He takes a deep breath, "I always used protection, I swear to you," he tucks a stray hair behind my ear, "There was the time after my dad died, the night you told me you were on birth control, and then she showed up at my hotel the night of the break-in."

He lowers his head and closes his eyes. Every word he's spoken is like a knife into my heart. I'm gutted. By his posture, he's waiting for me to run away. And the thought is in my mind, but I pushed him into telling me this. The masochist inside me felt this was all necessary. My inner romantic is scowling at me.

FORSAKING ALL OTHERS

My voice comes out quieter than I intended, "So, the night of the break-in, when I called you—she was there?"

He nods and I finally ask the question I've held inside for over six weeks, "The night of the accident—was it intentional? Did you mean to run that light?"

CHAPTER FIFTEEN
David

Her question shocks me. I'm not even sure what sound I make as I grab onto her arms. *My beautiful girl thinks I caused the accident as a way to get rid of her?*

I swallow hard, "Baby, you really think I'm capable of something like that? You think I would knowingly put you in danger?"

She uses her fingers to brush away the tears on her cheeks, "David, I don't know what to think. It's a lot to process, you know? I'm not accusing you of anything…I'm just trying to make sense of all of it."

I stand up and pull her into me, resting my chin on her head. "I was messed up after getting that phone call. Here I thought I'd been careful and she drops that bomb on me. The night of the break-in, after you called me, I was done. I didn't want to be that man anymore. I thought we'd find our ground again, you and me, and then she told me she was pregnant. I was thrown—I was backtracking in my mind, trying to work out the timing. When I thought I lost you—Beth, it damn near killed me."

Her shoulders shake as she cries and I pull her closer.

"David, I'm still trying to sort through fact from fiction. The wreck took a lot from me, and while I've recovered some of my memories, there's a lot that's still blank," she pauses as she wipes away more tears, "While I don't remember everything, I know you're it for me. You're the only man I'm ever going to love and call me selfish, but I don't want to share you with Jess."

I tilt her chin up until she's looking at me, "Then don't. I'm all yours—I've only ever been yours...I just lost my way. My heart fucking belongs to you though, babe."

She wraps her arms around my neck and pulls my mouth down over hers. I can't get enough of the taste of her, my hands have a mind of their own, stroking up and down her arms. I can feel the goosebumps and I know her feelings are just as intense as mine.

She pulls back, breathless, "So the sex thing... it's still off the table? Seriously?"

I grin at her, "Well, since we're calling off the divorce, I guess I can make an exception."

Her face falls and she takes a step back. Definitely not the fucking reaction I was expecting from her. Then she rips my heart out all over again.

"David, I don't want to make any rash decisions just yet. I'm still trying to get my bearings here. I want to know what that paternity test says before moving forward one way or another."

I clench my molars down so hard I expect them to crack. *What the actual fuck just happened here?*

"So, let me see if I understand this correctly. You want to take it slow and not make any rash decisions, but you want to have sex. Does that about cover it?"

She purses her lips in an attempt not to cry, "David, please—"

I try to keep my voice calm, but the rage is quickly surfacing, "No, Beth! You don't get to have it both ways. And a 'rash decision' is filing for divorce and having your husband served instead of trying to work things out—not the other way around."

She moves closer to me, "Do not yell at me! I want to know

what the paternity test says—as someone who would be responsible for helping you raise this kid, I am well within my rights to ask that from you."

I pinch the bridge of my nose, trying to regain control of the situation, "You said you loved me, that I was the only man you were going to love. When did that become contingent on a paternity test, Beth?"

She raises her voice, "I never said it was, David. I will love you regardless of what happens, but I am not going to stand by and have this physical reminder right in front of me—I would hate that poor child!"

I stand there, stunned. *Well, there it is.* I grab my keys and head for the front door.

Her voice calls after me, "That's right, David. Leave. That's what you're good at doing!"

My truck roars to life and I'm ready to snap. I've got to think. I want a drink more than I've ever wanted one, but I can't let myself go back down that rabbit hole. I feel like I'm driving around aimlessly when it hits me. I'm running. It's what I'm good at— Beth was right. I don't know how to face any of this head on.

I drive back to my hotel and begin throwing all my shit into a bag. I can't stay here anymore. I check out and immediately get back into my truck. There's only one place I can think to get rid of all of this tension.

I'm drenched in sweat and every muscle in my body is screaming, but I keep pushing myself further. I've spent the last two hours at the gym, trying to find something to work out my frustration. I ran for ten miles and felt nothing. From there, I began lifting, but found that it only ratcheted that anger up even more. Now, I'm beating the shit out of a punching bag—it's the only thing that feels satisfying right now.

"Mind if I join you?"

I look up to see Mike standing there. "How'd you know I'd be here?" I wipe the back of my arm across my forehead, sweat is pouring off of me.

He smirks, "You're not the only one who's good at stalking. I am a detective after all."

I stare at him, "You're stalking me now?"

He snickers, "No, dumbass," and holds up his cellphone, "*Find my Friends* app said you were here. Thought you might need some company after my comments earlier. I was out of line, man. Beth is a fantastic woman, recent behavior notwithstanding, and you'd be a fucking fool to let her go."

I nod at him, the closest either one of us will get to apologies. "What happens if that test comes back, saying I'm the father? What the fuck am I gonna do then?"

He wraps his hands with tape as he prepares to join me, "We cross that bridge when we come to it, man. Jess doesn't seem like a 'one man kind of girl' from what you've told me, there have got to be other men that could be on the hook for paternity here."

I slam my fist into the middle of the bag. "Yeah, but so far I'm the only fish on the line."

Mike holds the bag steady as I rain my fury down on it. "Dave, you ever think of hiring someone to follow her? See what she's up to? If you suspect she's not being honest with you, then what do you have to lose?"

I stop hitting the bag and step back, "That's why I'm friends with you, Mike. Always thinking like a detective."

He's right. I could hire someone to keep tabs on Jess—see what she does and who she's with when I'm not around.

We box until my arms are weak, the anger finally giving way to something else. Something I didn't think I'd have after this afternoon. Hope.

Beth

I hear David's truck as he goes speeding down the street. "Fuck!" I take a throw pillow off the couch and launch it across the room in anger. I immediately think of the baby, "Sorry, bean. Mommy shouldn't use words like that." I don't even know if the baby can hear me this early in the pregnancy, but I've apologized nonetheless.

The man makes me crazy with lust one minute and ready to murder him the next. I mean, in hindsight, it was probably a bit much to ask for a physical relationship without being willing to call off the divorce. I'm just not ready to withdraw everything yet, especially if there's even the smallest chance that he's the father of Jess's baby. In his mind though, it would just be one baby to work his life around—not two.

I know I need to tell him the truth, I can only hide this for so long. Just this morning, I woke up to a slightly rounded belly. To anyone who didn't know, I might just look like I had a big meal— but if David keeps coming around, he's going to put two and two together rather quickly. I'm vomiting all the time yet getting bigger…it doesn't take a rocket scientist to figure it out.

Maybe once the paternity test results come back, I'll tell him then. *That is, unless they prove that he's the father of Jess's baby.* Seriously, I'm surprised we haven't been offered our own reality show yet. There's only one way to calm my mind now.

I spend the next few hours cleaning the house because some things never change. The floors get the brunt of my frustration and soon they're gleaming in response.

I've just sat down in my chair, ready to relax, when the doorbell rings. I smile to myself—I knew he wouldn't stay gone for long. Now we need to call a truce or at least table the argument for a later date. I don't want to fight anymore. I rub my belly; this poor baby has been exposed to so much drama already. *I'm going to be better.*

I throw open the front door, "I knew you would—Landon? Why are you here?"

He gives me a curt nod and brushes past me to get inside, "Elizabeth. I'm sure you know why I'm here."

I shake my head, "No. I don't, and I think it would be best if you left."

He completely ignores that and begins pacing the living room. "We've got a little problem, Elizabeth. You told the special investigator something that wasn't true today."

I stare stupidly at him, waiting for him to elaborate. He begins running his hands through his hair almost obsessively while still walking laps around the couch.

"Elizabeth, you told the investigator that Katya and I broke up. That isn't true though. I don't know if it's a result of losing your memory in the car wreck or what, but Katya and I are still dating. Hell, I was actually about to propose when she went missing."

I'm sure my mouth is hanging wide open, I'm utterly dumbfounded right now, "But the coffee date—um, you asked me out for coffee?" *Was that a question or a statement?*

He sighs heavily and sits down on the edge of the sofa. I bite back the urge to tell him that he's sitting in David's spot. "Elizabeth, I am so sorry. I didn't mean to mislead you—I knew you had to be going through a rough time and I wanted to offer my support."

I lean back against the wall, my brain going ninety miles an hour in an attempt to make sense of what he's telling me, "What about the night I found out, Landon?"

"Do you love me?" I blurt the words out before I've fully had a chance to think it through. Remembering his actions at the bar that night makes me regret asking almost immediately.

He doesn't even hesitate, "Yes, and you love me."

He smiles at me and those dimples could be my undoing, "Um, about that. Katya knew about you—told me if I couldn't get you out of my system, she was leaving. She and I had only been back together for a few months,"

At this revelation, his eyes tear up, "I had you under my skin and I wanted to see if there was still a spark between us. When I went to your work and told you that we'd broken up—you blew me off. I was ready to wash my hands of the situation when I saw your friend out at a bar one night. She was bragging to someone about screwing your husband behind your back—"

I gasp in hurt. *She told people?* I blink quickly to dispel the tears that have started gathering in my eyes.

Landon jumps up and comes over to embrace me. I'm too shell-shocked to fight him.

He continues, "Once I knew the truth, I couldn't walk away from you. You are such a beautiful person inside and out—I couldn't imagine ever wanting to leave your bed. I didn't want to approach you until I had all the facts. By the time I made up my mind that you deserved the truth with or without proof, you'd been in the car wreck. I'll never forgive myself for keeping it from you—"

He folds his hands like he's praying and brings them under his chin, "I'm the reason you were in that car wreck. If I'd told you sooner, you wouldn't have been with him that night...you would've been safe."

I'm holding my hands over my mouth to stifle the sobs now. *What is wrong with me?* I ran back into David's arms so quickly without stopping to consider the consequences of my actions.

Landon pulls my hands away from mouth, "Hey, don't do that. Don't cry—" He pulls me into his hard chest again, "I think about what we could've been together...do you ever think of us? I mean—what we could've been if you found out about the lies sooner?"

I shake my head, "I've been so disgusted with my behavior. I cheated on my husband with you—I don't let myself go there because I don't recognize that woman."

He places a finger on my lips, running it lightly across. The effect is like a lightning bolt of pleasure, "Shhhh...do not shame yourself like that, Elizabeth. You were lonely. All I know is that if you were mine, you would never have had to look elsewhere—you know, had I not gone back to Katya. I would've spent every day letting you know how much you meant to me, giving you the attention you deserved."

In this moment, I can clearly see why I fell for him. His words awaken this longing within me, this desire to be cherished. His finger on my lip and arm around my waist have me ready to fall right back into him, even with his missing girl—fiancé...whatever she is. The thought of Katya is like a bucket of ice water being poured over me.

I talk around his finger, "Where do you think she is?"

He drops his arms, stepping away from me. "I don't know. I'm going to find her or die trying though. Will you help me?"

I swallow the lump in my throat, *"Help you?* How?"

He composes himself, "I've organized a search party for tomorrow afternoon. We're going to go door to door tomorrow morning, handing out flyers with her picture on them. We're meeting at Founder's Park at nine in the morning and then back there again around one. Please say you'll come."

I'm feeling a bit raw and my emotions are seriously all over the place right now. I want to say no, but the look in his eyes is so intense, that I find myself agreeing to meet him. His smile is so blinding when I agree, that I feel like I made the right choice.

I walk him out onto the front porch when he turns back, "Hey Elizabeth, it was really good to talk to you. I still owe you a cup of coff—"

The roar of an engine cuts off his words and I cringe. *This is very bad. I'm so screwed right now.* I close my eyes and let out a sigh as I hear a truck door slam.

"I swear to fuck, Landon. I thought I made myself pretty damn clear the last time you were on my property that it better be the last."

I pop one eye open, cringe still firmly in place, as I survey the scene in front of me. Landon's jaw is set and he's clenching and unclenching his fists, every muscle stretched taut.

Fuck. Fuck. Fuck.

I look over at David and he's in a similar stance. My eyes also catch our neighbor, Charles, standing stock-still in his front yard—

no doubt debating whether or not to call the cops for this little exchange.

I wave exaggeratedly, "Hey Charles! How's Nina?"

He reluctantly turns his attention over to where I'm standing, "Hey Elizabeth. Nina's fine—everything okay over there?"

I fake laugh and put on my best southern drawl, "Oh, you know how it is. Landon here forgot to return some tools he borrowed from David," I then stage whisper, "Not a good idea!"

It's so over the top, I'm certain he won't buy it. To my surprise, Charles nods wisely and looks over at David. "David, you're learning a valuable lesson here. Never let someone borrow something you expect to get back!"

David gives me a look before focusing his glare back on Landon. He answers Charles through a clenched jaw, "Don't worry, Chuck. Landon here won't be borrowing anything of mine ever again!"

I clap my hands together, "Well, that settles that. No one is going to be borrowing anything in the future. Landon, lovely to see you. David—can I have a word?"

Landon looks utterly destroyed, "I thought you filed for divorce. He's having a baby with your friend!"

David lets go of the front door handle and storms over to me. Before I can react, he's dragging me inside the house. "Stay here. I'm done dealing with his shit!"

I march back outside and get between the two of them. "Not here. Landon—I'll be there tomorrow. David—a word?"

Landon shakes his head and walks to the curb to get into his SUV. David pins me with a look that would wilt flowers. I turn away from him and go back inside before we draw another crowd. He follows, slamming the front door behind him—the glass rattles so hard, I'm afraid it's going to break.

"You'll see him tomorrow? What the fuck is that? I leave for a few hours and what—he's back in our bed?"

I exhale and spin on my heel, "What did you just say to me, David Greene?" My voice has risen several octaves in the process.

"You heard me, Beth. Are you fucking him again?"

My hand connects with his face and the sound is so loud that it startles me. He draws back in surprise, his eyes blazing with rage.

"How dare you, David. How. Fucking. Dare. You!" My voice wavers and then I feel tears hitting my cheeks.

The fight immediately goes out of his eyes and he sinks down into a dining room chair. "Jesus, Beth. I just accused you of being a whore. Please don't cry. I'm sorry."

I sink down until I'm sitting on the hardwood floor, my head resting on my knees. "You c-can't do that to me, David. It's n-not fair. If you automatically assume the worst—how are we going to make a life together?"

By the time I leave the gym, I feel much more in control of the anger. I was going to have to stick to my word and take things slow. I just needed to pull back and refocus my efforts. We had a lot of hurt between the two of us and I couldn't expect her to just move through all of that overnight.

It killed me to think that she was basing her future with me on the results of a paternity test though. If I could just get her to remember why we fell in love—why we're good together—maybe she'd choose me all over again, regardless of what the test said. I've got an idea of where to start as I turn onto our street.

And then I see *him* in my front yard.

All the good work in the gym—gone. I'm practically growling with anger when I shove the gear shift into park. Beth closes her eyes, bracing herself for the storm I'm about to bring.

I'm out of the truck and slamming the door shut before approaching him. The son-of-a-bitch has a fucking grin on his face. *I'm going to kill him.* "I swear to fuck, Landon. I thought I made myself pretty damn clear the last time you were on my property that it better be the last."

I'm pleased to see the grin disappear, but before I can settle things between us, Beth is yelling out to Chuck across the street. I quickly realize she's trying to divert his attention from what's about to go down, but I have a sudden urge to laugh.

She's made up some godawful story about Landon borrowing my tools and not returning them—I don't even know how she came up with it. There's a muscle twitching near Landon's jaw and I can't decipher if he's amused or ready to throw a punch. In the meantime, I keep a wary eye on him.

When Chuck calls out a warning about borrowing things, all humor ceases. It hits way too close to home for me.

My jaw clenches in frustration, "Don't worry, Chuck. Landon here won't be borrowing anything of mine ever again!"

Beth catches my eye and I can see worry etched all over her face. She claps her hands together and forces a smile. "Well, that settles that. No one is going to be borrowing anything in the future. Landon, lovely to see you. David—can I have a word?"

Landon decides now is the time to speak up. I'm pissed that she told him about filing for divorce. I feel as though my body is humming with rage as I pull Beth inside the house. I'm about three seconds away from decimating this fucker and I don't want her to witness it.

I warn her, "Stay here. I'm done dealing with his shit!"

As usual, Beth does what Beth wants and she follows me right back outside. She gets in between us and sends Landon on his way. I can't even think straight as I walk back inside—is she going to call him up to come over every time we fight? She's cut deep with her actions and I'm ready to return the favor.

I snap at her, "You'll see him tomorrow? What the fuck is that? I leave for a few hours and what—he's back in our bed?"

She stops walking and turns on me, her voice getting higher after each word. "What did you just say to me, David Greene?"

The words come out in a snarl, "You heard me, Beth. Are you fucking him again?"

FORSAKING ALL OTHERS

Her hand comes up out of seemingly nowhere before meeting my face. I'm shocked and for a second, the rage is deafening. Then, just as quickly as it came, it's gone.

She responds, "How dare you, David. How. Fucking. Dare. You!" I'm certain she's about to go on a tirade when I see the first couple of tears fall.

What the hell am I doing?

I sit down into a chair, the full weight of my words hitting me in the face just as she did. "Jesus, Beth. I just accused you of being a whore. Please don't cry. I'm sorry."

She slides down the wall until she's sitting on the hardwood. "You c-can't do that to me, David. It's n-not fair. If you automatically assume the worst—how are we going to make a life together?"

The minutes seem to lengthen in the silence. I go over and sit down in the floor next to her, my sore muscles protesting. I take her hand in both of mine, my fingers make little circles over her soft skin.

"I left here earlier because I was pissed off that you'd still go through with the divorce if it turns out I'm the father. I went to the gym and tried to process everything you said. I still couldn't imagine why you would deny yourself what you want because of one person," She opens her mouth to speak and I lightly place my finger against her mouth.

"Let me finish. It wasn't until I pulled up and saw Landon that it clicked. I love you, Beth. Hell, I'd kill for you if needed, but I won't share you with him. I get it—you won't share me with her either. So, we're at an impasse here. What do we do?"

Beth pulls her hand from mine and my heart is fucking free-falling through the floor beneath me. I'm surprised when she grabs onto my shirt and pulls me into her, resting her wet cheek on my chest. "Landon came by—"

I cut in, "Hey, you don't owe me an explanation—"

She haphazardly brings her hand up to my mouth and holds it there. "Shhhh…let me finish. Landon came by because of the alibi witness statement I gave. Apparently, he and Katya broke up for a while, but when he knew I was getting back with you—he went back to her. I gave a statement that contradicted that…I don't know, I guess I'm still forgetting things from before the wreck. He said he was going to propose and then he asked me to help him find her. He's organized a search party. That's why he said he'd see me tomorrow."

I sit in silence, her fingers still pressed to my lips. She wasn't running back to him. It's the only answer I need. I nip at one of her fingers and she seems surprised to find that they're still pressed to my mouth. She's been crying so hard that her eyes appear to be glowing blue.

I use my hand to tilt her splotchy face up toward mine. I don't know what we're going to do or how we're going to make it through this—all I know is that she's never looked more beautiful than she does in this moment.

"I love you too." Her voice is quiet, but her words are weighted. *Am I okay with loving her for as long as I have her?* Could I love her enough to overcome the obstacles?

She brings her hands up and cups my face in hers, "I'm gonna love you for as long as I have you, David. I just want to enjoy every moment we've got—no more fighting."

Her words echo my thoughts. *That's got to mean something.* I don't have time to dwell on it any longer because she presses her lips against mine and all rational thought ceases.

FORSAKING ALL OTHERS

It takes a lot of effort to not lose myself in her mouth. I need to stay in control. I'm not getting her into bed until we reach some sort of resolution here. The problem is, when she kisses me like this, there's nothing I want more. I reluctantly pull away when her hands find the hem of my shirt and start inching their way up.

"Can I take you to dinner?"

She sputters with laughter, "You really think that food is what you want right now?"

I groan, "No—I want you," Her eyes light with desire before I continue, "but I meant what I said earlier. I want it to be right between us. So, dinner it is."

CHAPTER SEVENTEEN
Beth

He's trying to kill me. I mean, what else could he be trying to do? My hormones are all over the place and just when I think he's going to give in, he pulls back.

I'm breathless and he's got a cocky grin on his face. Yeah, David knows exactly what he's doing to me. He gives me another quick kiss before he goes to shower. Once he leaves, I have a sudden desire to cry again. I need to get these emotions in check.

I freshen up my makeup and pull my hair up as he moves effortlessly around me, grabbing a shirt from his closet. He comes back out, the towel slung low around his hips, and my mouth goes dry. The water beads down his body and traces over every muscle.

"You almost ready?" His words snap me out of my trance and I realize I'm staring blankly into the mirror watching his every move.

"Y-y-yeah…I'm good." I put the cap back on the lipstick before realizing I never put it on. I take the cap off again and focus my attention on applying it carefully. I can see him watching me as I line my lips, his gaze is almost as intense as mine was. I snap the cap on and he blinks rapidly. *Two can play this game.*

David is still standing in his closet, a shirt wadded up in his hand. I look at him innocently, "You going to wear clothes to dinner or just the towel?"

He glances down and shakes his head as if to clear his mind.

FORSAKING ALL OTHERS

Elizabeth-1, David-0.

"Yeah, I'm uh…gonna change in the bedroom."

I wink at my reflection when he closes the bathroom door and go into the closet to find something to wear.

I come out a few minutes later in a black one shoulder kimono dress and strappy heels. It was the only dress that was loose enough to disguise the fact that I'm carrying a tiny human inside me.

He's watching *Sportscenter* when I walk into the living room so he doesn't notice me right away.

"Do you care if I drive? I'm a little wary of going out to dinner with you behind the wheel, if you know what I mean." I laugh as I say it, but I'm only slightly kidding.

"You let me drive you to lunch! You don't trust my driving now, Beth?" He reluctantly peels his eyes from the television to answer me and I get the privilege of watching him open and close his mouth like a fish out of water.

I grin wickedly at him, "That was lunch, not dinner. I think it's better if I drive. You coming?"

"You don't even know where we're going!" He calls after me as I open up the garage and climb into the driver's seat of my SUV.

I gesture to the passenger seat and he gives me a resigned look before getting in. I turn and smile at him, "Where to, boss?"

He rolls his eyes at me, but I can tell he's amused. "*Nick's*. I wanted it to be a surprise, but someone here in this car is a control freak."

Nick's…where it all began. No ulterior motives there, David. Nope.

I give him a fixed grin, "Great!"

I've just turned off our residential street when his hand reaches across and rests on my knee. "This is nice, Beth. Just you and me."

I smile and agree as beads of sweat trail down my spine. *How can his touch affect me like this?*

We reach the restaurant and find a parking spot in the crowded lot. David comes around and opens my door before grabbing my hand as we make our way across the gravel. This simple act is stirring up a lot of memories—the only problem is that I'm still unsure of when the memories occurred.

The air-conditioning is going full blast once we step inside, but with my husband's hand on the small of my back, I'm burning up inside. *Once we reach the bar he leans into me so I can hear him over the crowd, "I'm David, by the way." He extends his hand for me to shake. I grin up at him (that's all I seemed capable of doing since I met him- grinning like a fool) and lean back into him, "David, I'm Elizabeth. It's a pleasure to meet you."*

I sigh at the memory and David looks at me questioningly. "You okay, babe? Want to grab a table while I grab us some drinks?"

I nod before realizing that he'll expect me to drink. *Shit!* "Why don't you get the table and I'll get the drinks—maybe find something on the patio." I wink at him, rivulets of sweat on my back are making my dress stick to me.

"Yeah? Okay, but I'm not wearing an undershirt tonight so try not to spill!" I turn back to the bar when I feel his arms wrap around my waist. He nuzzles my neck and whispers in my ear, "Do you even know what I want?"

Me? Is it me? Please let it be me.

My heart is hammering in my chest when he gestures to the bar and I realize he's referring to his drink order.

My words become jumbled up in my mouth and it takes me a second to compose them into an actual sentence. "Y-yeah, a Shiner

FORSAKING ALL OTHERS

like usual. R-r-right?" *C'mon tongue, work!*

He steps closer to me as someone squeezes through the crowd, his eyes never breaking contact with mine. There's such an intensity when he looks at me like this, it makes it harder to think clearly.

He smiles at me as though he's amused, "Yeah, babe. I didn't know if you'd remember."

I did remember. I'm mentally giving myself a pat on the back when I realize I still have to figure out my drink situation. He squeezes my arm before pushing through the crowd and out onto the patio.

The bartender finally notices me and I shout out David's order. As he brings it over, I lean in closer, "Hi. I'm pregnant. Is there any way you could get me a *Malibu* and pineapple, but make it virgin?"

He looks perplexed, "So, you want pineapple juice and a lime wedge?"

I force out a laugh, "Yeah. That." *Seriously?*

He brings it back over and I give him my card to start a tab, "Thanks—and if a sexy man in a gray shirt comes up...he looks kind of like Daryl Dixon from *The Walking Dead*—well, can you continue to make mine virgins and not tell him. Like a secret?"

He agrees, but walks away shaking his head. He must think I'm insane. Hell, I'm starting to think I'm insane.

I use my back to push open the patio door, carefully holding both drinks in my hand. I'm almost halfway across the patio when I see him. He's sitting at the same table as when we first met and I'm once again hyperaware of my heart beating out a steady rhythm in my chest. I am about three steps away from him when I realize that I was focused on him and not the deck slats. My heel slips in perfectly, but this time I remain upright.

"Shit." I mutter the curse aloud and he turns around to face me.

"I had a feeling that if I sat here long enough, I'd end up rescuing a beautiful woman," He takes both drinks and places them on our table before dropping to his hands and knees to free my shoe. He looks up at me with that cocky grin and his southern accent is all of a sudden so much stronger, "You need some assistance, little lady?"

I playfully punch his arm, "I'm fine." I grab the red straw and suck down some of my drink before realizing it really is just pineapple juice and I'm going to remain painfully sober.

He takes a swig of his beer while glancing at the outdoor menu, "Feels like old times, yeah?"

I take another drink, still alcohol free, before answering, "Yeah, I've gotten a lot of flashbacks since we stepped inside. It's weird—David?"

He looks up at me expectantly, "Yeah?"

I take a deep breath, "What was I like…before?"

He takes another drink before asking, "How do you mean?"

I sigh, "I mean you've told me that the anxiety attacks were a recent thing, but I just wonder what I was like—I guess I just remember a lot of the bad stuff from before and I want to know if I'm more than that person."

He moves his chair closer to mine and grabs my hands, "You were always more than that, Beth. You know, I thought you changed because I was gone so much. You were laid back, but you didn't let me off the hook when I messed up. Before the accident and the affairs, you were a lot like you are now."

I focus on the way his hands dwarf mine as he talks. "What about when I was a kid? I remember going to therapy when we moved here. Is that true?"

FORSAKING ALL OTHERS

He nods, "Yeah, from what you've told me, it was just a handful of times. I don't know what you expect me to tell you— we've both had our ups and downs, but I've loved you no matter who you've been."

I squeeze his hand and offer to get us another round, as my mind is in need of a reprieve. David tries to stand up to go, "Babe, let me take care of that."

I smile patiently, "Well, I need to go to the bathroom, so you gonna take care of that for me as well?"

He shakes his head and smiles before sitting back down in his chair. "I'll be right here."

I grab us another round after coming out of the bathroom. The bartender recognizes me so I'm spared from embarrassing myself again. I've just turned from the bar when I get the feeling someone is watching me. I look around the crowded room, but don't see any faces I recognize. I shrug it off and carry our drinks outside.

CHAPTER EIGHTEEN
Beth

I manage to time my bathroom breaks perfectly the rest of the night to where I'm in charge of getting drinks. It's weird watching someone else drink to the point that they're tipsy while you remain stone cold sober.

David got more animated with every beer and at one point pulled me to my feet to dance on the patio. Thankfully, it was more like swaying in one spot as I was not looking forward to getting reacquainted with the deck.

He held me tight and sang the words in my ear—something about reminding the other person of how their love used to be. I didn't know who either of the singers were, but the song was beautiful.

Was that us?

Were we settling for good and not great? I found myself so caught up in the song that I began singing the words, 'remind me' back to him during the chorus. I opened my eyes to see that we were the only ones dancing and more than one person was staring, but I didn't care.

I realized once we sat back down that David may have had one too many and decide it's time to cash out our tab and get him home. *Home.*

Well, I guess he would have to stay at the house, I didn't know where his hotel was and I doubt he'd be willing to tell me. I pay the tab so we can be on our way.

"Did you just buy my drinks?" His voice is slightly slurred.

"Yes, I sure did. You're a terrible date—I bet you expect me to drive you home now."

His face falls, "Beth, I'm sorry. We got to talking and I lost track of how many I had."

I place my hand on his cheek, "Stop, I'm kidding. Let's get you home."

As I lead him to my car, he speaks up, "Maybe I'm not drunk. Maybe," at this he hiccups, "Maybe I just wanted your arms around me." He nods as if to reinforce what he's just said, but it looks more like he's about to doze off.

I laugh and open the passenger door for him, even going so far as to buckle him in. This is not how I saw the night going, but as I can't remember ever experiencing this before with him—I'm not even mad.

Once we get home, I get him into our bed—holding back when I help him out of shirt and jeans. He's out by the time his head hits the pillow, so I leave a couple of aspirin and a bottle of water on the nightstand.

I don't know how long I stand there, watching his chest rise and fall steadily, but it feels like a lifetime. I grab his clothes to take to the hamper, but change my mind at the last minute and keep the shirt. I wash my face and change into it. It hits me mid-thigh and I'm immediately enveloped in the smell of him.

I breathe deeply and sigh happily, my inner romantic nods her approval, while my brain is flashing warning signs. I choose to ignore it and climb into bed next to David. I curl my body around his and fall asleep almost instantly.

I dream I'm on a small boat in the middle of the ocean, being tossed helplessly by the waves. The feeling of being sea-sick is overwhelming. When I open my eyes, it's still dark and the clock shows that it's only three in the morning. I groan because the feeling of seasickness didn't go away when I woke up. David is still dead to the world, his arm draped across me. I disentangle myself carefully so I don't wake him. I move quickly, but stealthily through the dark house, my hand pressed over my mouth. I make it to the guest bathroom just in time to throw up pineapple juice onto the tile floor.

I clean up the mess once I'm done getting sick, but just as soon as I finish, another round of vomiting starts. When it's over, I go to the kitchen and grab a bottled water from the fridge. I take a tentative sip and immediately run back to the bathroom.

This is bad.

I've dealt with morning sickness for the last month, but it's never been this severe. I try taking smaller sips of water, but nothing stays down. I've thrown up so much that my throat feels raw and it hurts to swallow.

I've taken my pregnancy symptoms in stride up until this point, but if someone walked through that bathroom door and offered to carry the baby to term for me, I'd sign up in a heartbeat. I'm curled up in the fetal position with my face pressed against the cool tile when I feel the urge to vomit again. I throw up the little bit of water I drank, but my stomach is otherwise empty.

I'm just resigning myself to living out the remainder of my pregnancy on this bathroom floor when I hear hurried footsteps.

"Beth?" David is standing in the doorway in just his

underwear, somehow looking better than I do in spite of all that he drank, "Baby, I heard you getting sick. Are you okay?"

I moan in response and lay my face back against the tile. He grabs a washcloth and runs it under the faucet. Then, he's on his knees, wiping my face and neck with it. "What time is it?" My voice is raspy.

"Just after five. I woke up and didn't know where you were until I heard you get sick. Guess you drank too much."

I nod, even though it hurts my head to do so. He gets up and walks out while I resist the urge to watch him go.

He returns a few minutes later with a small bowl and a fruit punch Gatorade. He lowers the bowl and I realize it's Cheerios. *David's infamous hangover cure.* I'm amazed that I recalled it, all things considered.

"Try a couple of these and then take a drink. We'll get you fixed up in no time."

I grab a couple and pause, "How are you even functioning right now? You drank more than me." *And mine were non-alcoholic!*

He smiles, "I guess I'm not a lightweight like you, babe." He strokes the hair off of my face before his gaze travels downward, "You're wearing my shirt?"

I nod, very slowly.

"My shirt and nothing else?"

"Not the time, David. Not the time." I pop the Cheerios in my mouth, willing my body to not reject them.

He exhales sharply, "Right. Go ahead and take a drink."

I've just finished taking a drink when I feel everything coming right back up. I lean forward and get sick again. This process continues until I'm falling asleep in between episodes. David tries to wake me up to get me to take a drink, but it requires too much effort.

"Beth—open your eyes and look at me." His tone is sharp, so I begrudgingly open one eye. He's crouched over me, worry etched across his face.

I close my eyes again, *I just need five more minutes, Mom.*

"Open your eyes, baby."

I try to open my mouth to tell him to let me sleep, but it's too hard. Maybe he can just read my mind. I begin vomiting again, but can't move so I end up getting sick on the rug.

David lifts me up off the floor and carries me back to our bedroom. He gently places me on the bed and begins throwing on clothes. I close my eyes again, sleep beckoning me as he opens and shuts various dresser drawers.

"Here. Let's get these on you."

I startle awake as he struggles to get a pair of sweatpants on me. He manages to get them up around my waist with no help from me before lifting me off the bed and carrying me out to his truck. He reclines the seat so I'm not fully sitting up and buckles me in.

"Where're we going?" The words all run together, like my tongue is refusing to cooperate.

He glances over at me as he backs out of the driveway. "I think you have alcohol poisoning. I'm getting you to a hospital!"

Hospital?

No.

He'd find out I was pregnant. I had to force my muddled mind to think of a solution.

"No. Just let me sleep it off."

He shook his head and drove faster. I close my eyes to think and am immediately startled awake by him opening my door.

What? We just got in the car.

David unbuckles me and lifts me effortlessly into his arms and I see that we're at the hospital already. He rushes me through the automatic doors and over to the registration desk.

I try to pick up my head, but it lolls back onto his shoulder. My body weighs too much right now.

"—drank too much last night—can't stop vomiting..."

I feel the urge to vomit as he's talking and a quick-thinking nurse grabs a blue bag and shoves it into his hands. I should feel some sense of embarrassment that I'm puking in an emergency room full of people, but I'm beyond caring right now.

One of the nurses goes to find a doctor before coming back to the desk. I manage to hear something about orders for a toxicology screen. That same nurse asks if they can get a urine sample on me and I give her a panicked look before she continues, "I'll get a female nurse to help her."

David looks ready to argue with her until I place a hand on his chest, "Please..."

They bring a wheelchair out for me and a female nurse pushes me through some double doors and into the nearest bathroom. Once the door clicks shut, I find the solution I was looking for in the truck earlier.

"I-I'm pregnant..."

Her eyes widen in understanding, "And you drank too much alcohol last night?" She's working very hard to keep the judgment out of her voice.

"N-no," I sigh the words, "I have morning sickness, but this is the worst of it so far."

She nods at me and then cracks the door, "Barb? A word?"

An older woman walks in, her face giving the impression that she doesn't take anything from anyone. The nurse fills Barb in on the situation and she gives me an appraising look.

"So, I take it the man out there doesn't know this?"

I nod, my mouth is like the Sahara.

"Is he not the father then?"

I sigh, "He is. I just haven't figured out how to tell him that. We're sort of having problems right now."

She nods seriously, "Is now the time you want to tell him?"

I shake my head vigorously, the action nearly doubling me over in pain.

Barb turns back to the nurse, "Okay then. Let's get the urine sample and then get her into a room. I'll find out who our on-call obstetrician is this morning and be right back."

The nurse helps me with the urine sample and then Barb comes back. "Dr. Westland is on call right now—he wants to get an IV started, since it's obvious that she's severely dehydrated. He wants an ultrasound done as well."

When my eyes go round, she amends, "We'll have your um—"

"Husband." I supply helpfully.

"Perfect. We'll have your husband fill out some paperwork and financial forms while we do that."

They don't take me back to the waiting room, but into an exam room where both nurses help me into a gown and then through another round of vomiting.

They start an IV of fluids and Zofran to stop the vomiting while waiting on the doctor. David comes in a few minutes later and brings a chair over to the side of the bed.

"Back here again. I'd hoped you and I were done with hospitals for a little while—especially after the last time."

I close my eyes and nod, "Me too."

He leans over and grips my hand in his, "I've got to take better care of you."

His words break my heart because he thinks that not only was he responsible for the car wreck, but for me being sick right now too.

I mean, he kind of is responsible for the sickness...

Thanks, logic.

The nurse comes back in not long after and takes David to fill out the insurance paperwork. Once he's gone, the on-call obstetrician comes in and performs an ultrasound. My little gummy bear has changed in just over a week and is dancing around as though all is well.

The heartbeat is strong and I find a weight is taken off of me. I feel like I can finally relax, knowing that he or she is okay. He gives me a prescription for anti-nausea medication just as I belatedly remember that my doctor gave me one as well at my visit last week. I stuffed it down in my purse, instantly forgetting it. He uses the term hyperemesis gravidarum and urine ketones—all of which mean nothing to me until he breaks it down in layman's terms. Dr. Westland tells me that if I feel morning sickness to this magnitude again, to come straight to the hospital so they can give me fluids and monitor the baby. He assures me that he'll send everything over to my doctor for her records before leaving the room to see other patients.

David comes back about thirty minutes later (Man, do they know how to stall) and we sit in comfortable silence together, his hand firmly clasping mine. The IV fluids and medicine do wonders for me. My body gives up its fight and lets me rest peacefully.

CHAPTER NINETEEN
David

Watching her rest is such a relief. She smiles in her sleep and I wonder if she's thinking of me. I'd like to think she is, given all the hell she's put me through in the last six hours.

I woke up to a full bladder and an empty bed. My first thought was that she took the guest room, the very idea of it pissing me off. I'd wanted to wake up to her in my arms, to have some small feeling of normalcy with her.

I shouldn't have been drinking last night, not after I'd done well enough without it. I allowed the stress of our situation to cloud my judgment and once again found myself in over my head. I was amazed she could keep up with me though. Normally, Beth kept herself to a two-drink maximum. The funny thing is, she seemed completely sober when we left to go home.

Just as I flushed the toilet, I could hear the sounds of her retching from down the hall. I didn't think, I just ran to her.

She was a ghostly shade of white even against the porcelain of the toilet. I tried asking her questions, but she could only answer me in moans. I tried wetting her face with a cold washcloth and when that didn't work, I went with my never-fail hangover cure. I felt that if I could get her to eat a few dry Cheerios and get some electrolytes in her, she'd bounce back.

I was distracted from my worrying when I realized she was in my shirt. I don't know, but just the thought of it had me ready to puff up my chest and proclaim to the world that she was mine.

I stroked the damp hair back off of her forehead while taking her in. "You're wearing my shirt?"

She looked up at me and nodded her head.

"My shirt and nothing else?" My heart was pounding and I ached at the thought of being inside of her.

She must've picked up on my thought process because she weakly said, "Not the time, David. Not the time."

I watched her eat the dry cereal and wash it down with some Gatorade. I thought she'd be right as rain soon.

Turns out, I was wrong.

If anything, my cure made her sicker.

She continued to vomit and when she started falling asleep immediately afterward, worry turned into something more. *Alcohol poisoning.* It didn't make sense though. She'd seemed fine last night. I told myself I was jumping to conclusions—that I just needed to give her more time to recover.

I leaned against the counter and watched her, praying the signs wouldn't be there. She started shivering violently so I moved over her again, calling her name. She wasn't as responsive as I would've liked and her lips had a blueish tint to them. When she threw up on the rug, I was convinced we needed help.

Trying to dress an unconscious adult was not my idea of a good time, but considering that she did the same for me the night before, I couldn't complain.

I felt like I ran every red light trying to get Beth the help she needed. She'd tried arguing with me in the driveway, but her words all ran together—yet another sign she was still intoxicated.

Thankfully, the nurses seemed to take her situation seriously as well. The one nurse, Barb, immediately found the doctor so they could get labs ordered. They took her back and ran all the tests, but it wasn't until just now—watching her sleep that I feel I can exhale.

I grabbed her purse as we ran out the door in case they needed her identification, and I can hear her phone vibrating from across the room. I go and get it, trying not to wake her.

Landon.

It's like the guy can't take a hint. He's called five times in a row. The phone starts vibrating again in my hand and I step out into the hall, closing the door softly behind me.

"Hello?"

"Who's this?" Even over the phone he sounds condescending.

"Who the fuck do you think it is?" I hiss the words into the phone, earning myself a dirty look from the nurse's station.

"Why are you answering Elizabeth's phone? Where is she?"

I walk down the hallway, out of earshot of anyone. "It's none of your fucking business where she is!" I've got a death grip on her cell phone right now.

He laughs, "Geez Davey, calm down! I'm just wondering why she isn't here right now. She said she'd help with the search party today, but she never showed up. Hence, why I'm wasting my breath talking to you."

I clench and unclench my jaw, working to keep my voice low. *Davey? Oh, hell no.*

"She's sick and won't be coming today. That's all you need to know."

His tone becomes worried, "Sick? What's going on?"

I should hang up, but I can't help myself. *I'm a prick.* "I guess she drank too much when we were at dinner last night. I woke up in our bed alone in the middle of the night—poor thing was sick in the guest bathroom. Don't worry, Landon. She's in good hands."

He protests, "What?—Why were you over there? You're getting a divorce! She said—"

I cut him off, "Great talking to you, Landon. Good luck finding your *fiancé*."

I mash the end button. *Fucker.*

I'm gonna need a few laps around the floor to calm myself down.

Beth is starting to wake up when I make it back to the room. She gives me a sleepy smile and my heart turns over in my chest.

"How you feeling, baby?"

She nods, "Good...my mouth is still really dry." She sounds pretty hoarse. I go and grab her some ice chips after clearing it with one of the nurses.

I spoon a few into her mouth, getting comfortable on the bed in the process.

Beth starts giggling and I give her a puzzled look, "What's so funny?"

She tries to compose herself, "You—I'm just laughing at the picture we must make. The big, tattooed alpha spoon-feeding ice to his invalid wife."

I spoon more ice into her mouth and give her a stern look, "My dad would've done this for my mom."

She gives me a sad smile, "Yeah, he would've. He loved you and her more than anything else in this world, David."

I swallow hard at her words. "You."

She looks over at me, "What?"

I grab her hand, "You. He loved you too, Beth. So damn

much."

She quiets for a moment, continuing to eat the ice chips as I feed them to her.

"Did you love her?"

I freeze, the spoon stopped halfway to her mouth, "Who?"

Her voice comes out barely above a whisper, "Jess—did you love her? Is that why you um went to her?"

Why? Why can't we just have one moment where the past doesn't threaten everything?

I realize she thinks I ran to Jess because of her looks and I've never understood why she's never felt that she could measure up next to her. I've always thought Beth was sexy as hell, but she never agreed, especially if Jess was in the room. The implications of what I did extend beyond those three encounters. That's glaringly obvious to me right now.

I slept with the one person she measured herself against. I took those insecurities and validated them by my actions. I've hated myself for what I did to her, but this is an entirely new level of self-loathing.

I couldn't process my dad dying so I fucked her best friend? Why is it, that up until this point, I've thought we could move past everything? I am the last person she needs in her life.

What I'm about to tell her makes this worse, because I never felt anything toward Jess. She just happened to be at the right place at the right time—or wrong place at the wrong time, depending on how you look at it. If anything, I hated her. I hated that she would do that to Beth, but more than that I hated that she wasn't Beth.

"No. I never loved her. She was just there..." I don't know what else to say to make this better. Her eyes well up and she looks out the window, away from me. I realize I never wanted anything more than to be like my old man—in this moment, I'm the furthest thing from that dream.

CHAPTER
TWENTY
Beth

Luckily, my second hospital stay was short-lived. I immediately filled the prescription for anti-nausea medication and fell into bed upon arriving home. David said he had to take care of some things and left me to rest, but I knew the truth—he was punishing himself. After he admitted that Jess had been nothing more than convenient, the atmosphere in that small room changed.

And not for the better.

I didn't know whether I was crying tears of relief that he didn't love her or tears of hurt because he went to my best friend. *Former best friend.*

I also didn't know why I couldn't just enjoy a moment with my husband? It's like some part of me refused to let myself be happy, as if I didn't deserve it. I know he felt the same way too. I saw the way the light in his eyes was extinguished by my question.

He'd just finished telling me how much his dad loved me and I had to go and verbally hit him in the nuts for it. As if he needed reminding that he was not his father.

Why? Why am I so cruel to him?

As I lay there, wondering where David ran off to, I began to think that I must have a victim complex. Either that, or my level of masochism was through the roof. How could tearing my heart open all over again possibly help me heal and forgive?

FORSAKING ALL OTHERS

It's not until the following Friday when I realize I never showed up to help Landon. I realize this when I see his name flash across my cell phone screen.

"Hey, Landon—" He cuts me off before I can apologize.

"Elizabeth? Are you okay? I heard you were sick."

What? How?

"You did? Who told you that?"

"David did. I called you Sunday afternoon and he said you were sick, but that he was taking care of everything. He told me you called off the divorce and that he'd moved back in—I guess it surprised me."

I try to keep the anger from my voice, "Oh, he told you all that?" I need to change the topic and get back on neutral ground, "How did the search go for Katya? Any leads?"

He sighs, "Not a damn one. We're going to try to cover more ground tomorrow and Sunday if you want to join us. I could use any and all volunteers."

"Okay, I'll go. What time and where?"

He gives me the time and location before we hang up and I sit in silence at my kitchen table. I'm not mad that David told him that. No, what I'm mad about is the fact that I haven't seen or heard from the man since he dropped me off Sunday.

He tells Landon we're together, all but pissing on my leg it sounds like, but won't tell me. If he would've asked to move in, I would've said yes. As crazy as it sounds with an impending divorce on the table. I want him to prove me wrong. I want him to show me that we can work through this, but if he's going to pull a disappearing act every time something happens, there's no way.

I think back over the conversation we had in the hospital and cringe.

My words.

I've been pushing him away for the last few weeks. So, why am I surprised that he's finally listening?

I hold the phone in my hand, ready to call him. *It's not enough.*

I need to go find him, tell him I'm sorry.

I call up Mike, who picks up on the first ring. "Elizabeth, everything okay? Is David okay?"

I smile at his concern, "I'm fine, Mike. I was actually wondering if you knew where I could find David."

He's clicking something in the background, "Have you checked your app?"

I frown, "My what?"

He sighs heavily into the phone, *"Find my Friends*, Elizabeth. The app I had you and David download. Are you telling me you're still not using it?"

His words spark a memory. Right before the wreck he was on this kick about keeping tabs on his friends and family. I teased him mercilessly about his poor detective skills if he was relying on a phone app to know our whereabouts. Up until this point though, I've paid no attention to the thing whatsoever.

"Oh right...the app. Sure, I'll check that. Thanks, Mike!"

He continues rambling on, "Seriously, no one pays attention to anything I have to say. I'm try—"

I stop him, "Wait, so that means you must have Lauren on yours. Ooh la la. How's that going?"

The clicking sound stops, "Uh, I've got another call coming in. I'll talk to you later."

He disconnects before I can say anything further. *I'll have to ask Lauren about that later.*

I take the time to pull up the stalker app on my phone, fascinated with seeing where everyone is.

Mike is at the station.

Lauren is at the gym.

David pops up about seven miles away from me and my stomach gives a nervous flutter in anticipation.

What am I going to say?

I know if I think about it any longer, I'll lose my nerve, so I throw my phone into my purse and prepare to meet my fate.

I'm white-knuckling the steering wheel. I need to keep my head clear. I've gotten so caught up in his kisses and being near him, that I've forgotten we have real problems to work through.

So, first I'll apologize and then we can work through this mess. I won't act like a love-struck teenager around him anymore. He's right about one thing—we can't have sex until things are worked out and divorce is no longer an option. No more physical until we work out the emotional (I'm smiling at my own cleverness).

Right. Good plan.

I find the cross streets from the locator app and park in a dirt lot. I can see David's truck parked not too far from mine along with various other work vehicles. I get out and my heels immediately sink into the soft dirt. I sigh. I didn't quite think everything through.

Who shows up to a construction site in heels?

I get back into my SUV and look around for another pair of shoes. Luckily, there's a pair of cheap flip flops in the back seat. They're bright yellow and don't match my outfit, but they're all I've got.

A radio is blaring country music and people are shouting back and forth to each other as they work. I get more than a few curious glances as I walk past and I realize I must stick out like a sore thumb.

David's right in the thick of it, laughing with one of his employees as they frame out the building. The heat is blistering and I've only been out in it for a few minutes. I don't know how David is managing.

As if sensing my thoughts, he pulls his t-shirt free from his jeans and over his head. He mops the sweat off of his brow with the hem of it and then his crystal blue eyes meet mine.

The script in my head is forgotten.

All my plans? Gone.

My panties? Through the dirt beneath my feet and halfway to China.

He remains rooted where he is as if he can't allow himself to believe I'm really there.

I know I need to remember my reason for coming, but as I stand there with the breeze blowing my long hair, I only want one thing.

Him.

I don't wait for logic to return. I take off running across the dirt and jump into his arms. My legs go around his waist just as his hands come up to support me.

The whistles and catcalls begin almost immediately and I bury my face in David's neck as I'm blushing crimson.

"Beth?"

"Shhhh...I need to tell you something."

He waits expectantly, his arms tightly holding me in place.

"I'm sorry, David. For everything. I know you think I was comparing you to your dad the other day, but I wasn't. You are a great man in your own right. I'm sorry I didn't always see the best in you…I'm sorry that I allowed Landon into our lives. I'm sor—"

I'm trying to focus on his chest instead of meeting his eyes, so he has to lean down to get close to my face.

"Hey. Look at me. You think I haven't been home because I felt like you were comparing me to my dad?"

I nod, tears welling up.

He laughs and walks us away from the crowd. "Baby, I left because I'm no good for you. I've been fighting for us, but it wasn't until you asked me if I loved Jess that I realized the enormity of what I've done to you. I've watched you compare yourself to Jess for years and the instant things fell apart in my life, I went to her. Not you. A good man doesn't do that. You have every right to want to stay far away from me."

No.

I shake my head mutely, disagreeing with every word.

"You don't think we can make this right?"

David gently sets me onto the dirt, several of his employees are still very much invested in the soap opera we're playing out. He takes note of this and walks me back to my vehicle. Once we're hidden from prying eyes he answers me.

"Beth, I want you—I do. That makes me a Grade A prick. You deserve better…I guess it took me long enough to see it."

I blink rapidly trying to make my eyes stop watering. This is not how I saw this going. "So, there's no chance? I came all the way down here to ask you to move back in…and all of it was for nothing?"

He looks like he's been sucker punched. "You wanted to ask me to move back in? Even after all I've put you through?"

I sniff and open my car door, wishing the dirt would swallow me whole. "Not anymore, I guess."

I leave him standing in the dust that my SUV kicks up.

"So he's changed his mind all of a sudden?" Lauren pours another glass of wine as we sit on the patio, watching the sun sink lower and lower on the horizon.

I sip my sparkling water, a poor substitute in comparison. "I don't know, Laur. He's so hard to figure out—one minute we have this intense chemistry and he's begging for a second chance and the next he's pushing me away, saying I deserve better. The man is giving me emotional whiplash!"

She laughs and takes a long drink, "Beth, maybe he's taking all of your sadistic questions as a sign that you aren't ever going to move on. I mean, really, how can rehashing all the gritty details be helpful?"

I press my fingers to my forehead, massaging away the headache that's starting behind my eyes. "I just want everything out in the open—no more secrets. I don't want to run into her and leave feeling like she knows something I don't. With both of us being pregnant and seeing doctors in the same office, these are real concerns here."

Lauren nods, "You've got a point, but I think you've got to preface any conversation you two have with what you just told me. Let him know that you want the details in order to move forward— not to relive the past."

"Maybe I should just let my body do the talking. He doesn't seem to misinterpret that."

Lauren chokes on her wine and spends the next minute

coughing and fanning her tearing eyes. "Warn a girl before you go and say shit like that! And no, your idea sucks. Sex is not the answer, especially if you want to make this work in the long run."

I get up to refill my water when I hear the doorbell and a steady pounding on the front door. Lauren follows after me as I slowly walk toward it.

"Who is it?" I call out, a bit wary of answering given my recent history.

"Beth, it's me. I was wrong. I can't—"

I throw open the door before he can finish his sentence. He's standing there with his gym bag and several shirts still on hangers.

"You can't what, David?" I whisper the words, needing to hear him say it.

I watch his Adam's apple bob as he swallows, "I can't walk away from this—from you. Right, wrong—whatever—I'm fucking crazy about you. I'm willing to fight every damn day to prove that to you. I don't give a damn anymore if it's selfish to want this as badly as I do. I just want to come home to you. Does your offer still stand?"

I jump into his arms again. This time, he's ready for me and doesn't stop my mouth from meeting his.

CHAPTER
TWENTY-ONE
David

I'd spent the last five days kicking myself for leaving her. I couldn't get the hurt look she'd given me out of my head though. If there was ever a time for a do-over, now would be it.

If I could just change that night at the bar—No—if I could change how I ran my company in those early days...*If I'd listened to my dad,* she'd still be mine.

I snap back to the present when I realize Dr. Gregory—Alan—has asked me a question.

I give him an apologetic look, "I'm sorry?"

He smiles and leans back into his chair, "No worries, David. I am interested in where your head is at this morning though."

I sigh. *With her...it's always with her.*

"I'm just struggling. I know I fu—I messed up, but I want to fix it. I need her."

He nods and jots down a few notes, "Do you think that you might be putting Beth on a pedestal here?"

When he sees the anger on my face, he clarifies, "Now, don't get me wrong. A man should want to put his wife's needs above his own. What I'm referring to here is the fact that you say you need her. Do you think you're relying on her to fix what's broken? Could she even meet such impossible standards?"

I've got my hands folded like I'm praying, running them up and down my beard. I hadn't looked at it like that. If I just rely on

FORSAKING ALL OTHERS

Beth taking me back, is it really going to fix anything?

How would she ever trust me again?

I left his office and went right back to work, thoughts from my visit never leaving my mind. My guys must've thought I was pissed off, the way everyone steered clear of me. I can't say I didn't appreciate the silence.

I jumped in and began framing up the walls for what was going to be a restaurant. I felt like Lubbock could rival New York City with its abundance of places to eat, but jobs like this paid my bills so I'd never complain.

A few hours and several cases of near heatstroke later, I strip off my shirt and mop my face with it. It's almost time to call it a day. I'm not looking forward to spending another night alone. I checked out of that damn hotel room only to be right back in it the next day. Maybe I could call up Mike, see if he wanted to grab a bite—anything to keep me from sitting alone in my hotel room. If I sat there long enough, the thoughts of Beth were almost enough to drive me to buy out a liquor store and drown myself in whiskey.

I can feel her presence before I pull the shirt away from my face. I look up and meet her big blue eyes. She looks like a siren and I would happily let the sound of her voice drive me toward the rocks, if only because I'd be near her.

I want to run to her, but I hold back. I don't want to overwhelm her, especially when I don't even know why she's here.

Beth surprises me when she jumps into my arms. She almost knocks me over and I bring my arms around her for support, her long hair shielding us from everyone else.

I don't know what I expect, but it's certainly not an apology. I want to laugh because she thinks I left because of her comments on my dad. The guys are getting rowdy, so I walk away to give us some privacy.

Her eyes are filled with tears and I feel like that's all I'm capable of doing—making her cry. When I explain why I left and why she needs to stay away, she actually shakes her head as if to argue. I want nothing more than to fall back into a life with her, but I want to do it for the right reasons—two broken people picking up the pieces together—not me relying on her to fix everything.

"You don't think we can make this right?" Her question cuts deep, but I know what I have to tell her.

She deserves to be with someone who would never take her for granted. A man who'd never broken her trust. While I would fulfill the first one, I could never take back what I did.

I expect her to slap me again, I deserve her anger. What I don't deserve is what she says next.

"So, there's no chance? I came all the way down here to ask you to move back in...and all of it was for nothing?"

I feel like the air has been knocked out of my lungs. "You wanted to ask me to move back in? Even after all I've put you through?"

She gets into her car, wiping stray tears off of her face. "Not anymore, I guess."

I don't have a chance to think her words through before she leaves me in a cloud of west Texas dirt.

Fuck.

What am I doing?

I don't know how I manage to make it through the rest of the workday, but I do. I'm at war the entire time with my thoughts.

Guilt eats at me over the way we left things. I owe her an explanation for earlier—Hell, I owe her an explanation for everything.

FORSAKING ALL OTHERS

That's how I come to find myself standing outside my own front door, freshly showered and holding my heart in my hands.

On the way over, I thought that she'd probably end up slamming the door on me, I wouldn't have blamed her if she did.

I watch her face as I lay all my cards on the table and instead of slamming the door, she jumps into my arms.

I remember thinking that we'd just overcome the biggest hurdle in our relationship. Beth was mine. Permanently.

I had no idea of how cruel fate could be.

CHAPTER
TWENTY-TWO
Beth

Against the odds, David and I are finding our way back together. These last few weeks have felt like a marathon of couple's counseling sessions—we've tried to be as honest with each other about the past as we possibly could be.

No secrets—everything out in the open.

Well, almost everything.

I still haven't told David I'm pregnant.

I got a call from my doctor a few days ago while David was still home and I ended up taking it in the closet. The nurse apologized and told me they needed to push my appointment to September eighth due to scheduling conflicts. When I walked out of the closet, he was leaned up against the bathroom doorframe, giving me a puzzled look.

I told him it was Lauren and she had some personal stuff to discuss. By the look on his face, it was obvious he didn't want to know what sort of personal stuff.

The morning sickness has also almost completely gone away. I'm fourteen weeks today and I feel better than ever.

There's just one small problem.

My hormones.

Specifically, my libido.

I live with an incredibly sexy man. A man who has slept in the same bed as me every night since he moved home.

A man who will not put out no matter what I do to try and change that. He is somehow content while leaving me dangling from a cliff.

When I've approached the subject, he's said he wants everything to be right between us. I know that's not the only thing holding him back. It's the divorce.

I haven't called it off yet. I know I should, the timing just hasn't been right. I gave myself a one month deadline from the night he moved back in. I thought if we could survive a month of living under the same roof again and working through our issues, then I'd know for sure we were meant to be.

I just couldn't voice that to David. *I just told him he could move back in, but how could I tell him that it was a thirty day trial?*

I look up from the magazine I've been staring at while lost in thought, just as Lauren nudges me, "You alright? You've been quiet this morning."

I nod slowly at her, "Just tired."

She decided to use some of her paid time off to accompany me to my doctor's appointment so that I wasn't alone. I secretly think she was hoping that Jess would just so happen to be here again.

Jess.

Yet another reason I wasn't exactly ready to throw caution to the wind and work on living happily ever after just yet. Thankfully, she was nowhere to be seen this morning. I don't want to think of how she'd react when she found out David had moved back in.

I didn't see her at my last visit either—maybe she requested that her appointments be on a day I wasn't here. I'm not sure how often she sees her doctor, but David hadn't mentioned going with her again.

"Elizabeth Greene?" A nurse with a clipboard in her hands

scans the waiting room for me.

"Looks like we're up. Go on, I'll grab your purse."

They weigh me in and check my blood pressure. I'm finally starting to gain back a little of the weight I lost in the first trimester. My little baby bump has also grown and I've had to wear flowy tops in an effort to conceal everything just for a little bit longer.

I need the results of that paternity test now.

I want to be able to fully exhale and not feel like I'm holding my breath, waiting on the other shoe to drop. I want to fully give my heart back to the man who vowed to forsake all others, while loving and cherishing only me. I've been through hell and back, is it too much to ask for a happy ending?

As if the universe is answering my question, Jess turns the corner and almost walks right into us.

I sigh and look up at the ceiling tiles, "Seriously?"

The nurse, unaware of the drama that is unfolding, hands me a cup and directs me to the bathroom for a urine sample. Lauren is facing Jess head on and clenching her fists.

Jess looks from me to Lauren, "Hi."

Lauren holds up her hand, "Did I say you could talk?"

Jess's face darkens, "What did you just say to me?"

I bite back a laugh at the madness of the entire situation and pull Lauren away. "C'mon, Rocky. She's not worth it."

Lauren grumbles about it, but ultimately follows me.

As we make our way around Jess to get to the bathrooms, I'm painfully aware of her eyes homed in on my stomach. I self-consciously pull my shirt down and away from my body.

Does she know?

As if she can't help herself, Jess spits out, "He leaves and you let yourself go. I guess without me around to guide you, you've gone back to eating everything in sight." She gives me a big fake smile that quickly changes to horror when Lauren charges toward her.

"Y-y-you bitch!" Lauren spits out the words and I cringe. I really want to see my baby today. At the rate we're going, we'll be in the back of a police cruiser instead.

Lauren continues, "You may prance around like you're God's gift to men, but inside—you are as ugly as they come. I want nothing more than to beat the shit out of you right now. I'm sure my boyfriend could even make sure any charges you pressed were dropped as well, but I have a thing against hitting a pregnant woman. So, consider it your lucky day and turn the hell around before I change my mind."

She doesn't raise her voice, but her words are clear.

Jess opens her mouth again, no doubt wanting to push Lauren into an altercation, but I cut her off, "Jess, judging by this morning in bed, David is just fine with all of this." I gesture down my body as I say it and take pleasure in watching the color drain from her face. Maybe it's not the whole truth—I mean, we did wake up in the same bed, but that was the extent of it. She doesn't need to know that though.

Without another word, I turn and stalk toward the bathroom, Lauren racing to catch up with me.

"Oh my God, Elizabeth! Did you just say that?" She shuts the bathroom door and leans up against it. "That was amazing, did you see her face?" She dissolves into a fit of giggles that I can't help but join in on.

My legs are feeling a little wobbly after that confrontation. I'd really like the remainder of my pregnancy to remain stress free or I fear this baby is going to be born needing Xanax to function.

When the nurse gets us back into a room, Lauren excuses herself to make a call.

"Laur—" I warn. "Don't get into trouble please. Remember, you're too pretty for prison orange."

She smiles, "I swear…just a phone call. No covert missions. Although—I wonder if Mike could bring home one of those jumpsuits…we already have the handcuffs…"

My mouth drops open in shock.

"Cat got your tongue, Elizabeth? Do you need to play Candy Crush to block it out? That always works for me."

I swat at her arm as she ducks out of the room.

I change into the thin cotton gown and try to make myself as comfortable as possible.

The nurse comes back in a few minutes later, but Lauren is still M.I.A. though. I wanted to wait for her, but this nurse seems to be in a hurry.

She squirts lukewarm gel onto my stomach and grabs the wand. "Um, did you happen to see my friend out in the hall?"

She doesn't even make eye contact with me, "No, I sure didn't."

She presses the wand to my lower abdomen and thoughts of Lauren are forgotten. Gone is the gummy bear from before. This looks more like a baby. The nurse takes her measurements with clinical detachedness while I tear up and marvel at the screen.

I hear the door open and Lauren comes back in. She looks like she's seen a ghost.

"Lauren, are you okay?"

She nods distractedly and then looks over at the screen. "Is that it? Oh my goodness, it's like a real baby!"

I chuckle, "Well, it's not a dinosaur."

"The profile kind of looks like David's, don't you think?"

I study the screen closer and see that it does kind of resemble him. The nurse, in what I think is an attempt to help, switches the screen over to 3D and we both shriek in horror.

"Oh my God...it looks like an alien!" Lauren claps her hand over her mouth. "Elizabeth, I'm sorry. I shouldn't have said that. Your baby looks adorable."

I clasp her hand, "It does look a little strange right now. Hopefully, he or she will grow out of that."

Lauren points at the screen, "Looks like it's a he. Congratulations and Mazel Tov."

The nurse interrupts, "That's the umbilical cord. It's still a bit early to tell the sex."

Lauren nods thoughtfully, "Ah...I was thinking that was a bit longer than normal."

I laugh until tears pour down my cheeks again.

With Lauren in the room, everyone seems to lighten up a bit. Once she got Rose, the nurse, laughing—we were in the clear. Rose asked me questions about the baby and even asked if I had any special requests for ultrasound pictures. I asked if she could get the baby's foot and she happily obliged.

"Do you feel that?"

I looked over at Lauren, "Feel what?"

She pointed at the screen, "That. Do you feel the baby doing gymnastics in there?"

I laughed, "Not quite yet. The baby is only the size of a lemon." I stared at the screen longingly. Hopefully soon, I would though. That would make everything seem real.

Dr. Harper comes in soon after and looks over everything. "Well Elizabeth, everything looks good so far. Are you feeling better?"

I smile, "Once I remembered the medication, things were much better. I feel great now."

"I'm going to send you down to the lab for those tests—cfDNA and Quad screening. We talked about it a little the last time you were here. Is that still something you want to do?"

It hits me out of nowhere. I'm making all of these decisions without David. It's incredibly selfish to do that to him. *I've got to tell him the truth.*

I agree to the testing and Lauren joins me in the lab downstairs, both of us in a more somber mood. I look over at her worriedly checking her phone and pacing the small waiting area.

"Laur—what's going on with you? Did something happen?"

She stops and bites her bottom lip, "I-uh-I'm not sure. I'm still trying to figure that part out. I overheard Jess talking to someone in her room about testing and blood samples—it might not be anything, but I think she was getting labs for a paternity test today. Something just doesn't feel right though."

I take my hand and massage my temple, trying to ward off the headache that just popped up. "How did you overhear that? Were you spying on her?"

Lauren breaks eye contact with me and looks down, "No. I couldn't find the bathroom. I got lost."

I snort, "You couldn't find the bathroom we had literally just come from?"

"Nope. Got lost—Jesus, where is a lab tech when you need one? Shouldn't they be stabbing you with needles right about now?"

I wince, "When you put it like that, I'm not really sure I need these tests done."

She sits down next to me and grabs my hand. "Sorry. So, I lied. I just wanted to know what she was doing. I don't trust her—and can we take a minute to ask ourselves why you look more pregnant than she does? Isn't she like two months ahead of you?"

Feelings of inadequacy bubble up, "Good genes? The body of a supermodel? I don't know—take your pick."

She continues, ignoring me. "That's just it. She isn't showing at all. I've researched this and she should be showing—she's gotta be over twenty weeks pregnant by now."

I interrupt her musings, "How exactly did you research all of this?"

She looks at me seriously. "Google. You can research anything using that."

I purse my lips to keep from laughing, "You Googled pregnancy bellies? That's…that's interesting, Lauren."

"Don't take my word for it—look it up yourself. Not one person I saw had a flat tummy. Geez—are they going to come get you soon? I really want to have lunch sometime today!"

I laugh, "Are you sure you're not the one who's pregnant here?"

After what feels like an eternity, they call me back. The lab technician takes a lot more blood than I was expecting before promising me results within a week.

I briefly wonder how long it'll take for the results of the paternity test to come back. *How much longer will I have to hold my breath, waiting for a verdict?*

CHAPTER
TWENTY-FOUR
David

I'm home. Just a few months ago, I didn't know if I'd be able to say that ever again. Of all the things I missed, I think being in my own bed with my wife mere inches away was at the top of the list.

She insisted on helping Landon find Katya the day after I moved home and I had to grit my teeth to keep from losing my shit. I was going to have to trust her if I wanted this to work—didn't mean that I had to sit at home while she went though. I showed up and joined the damn search party as well. I was even nice to Landon—by nice I mean that I didn't hit the asshole in the face when he talked to her.

Beth never said it, but I think it meant a lot to her. So, every weekend since I moved home, we walked the streets and went door to door to find a missing woman, for a man that I detested. *Tell me that's not true love.*

She looks so much more relaxed than I remember seeing her in the past year. I have to remind myself that it's because we aren't leading double lives anymore.

I don't want to be naïve, but it feels like we're still in some "honeymoon phase." We're rebuilding our life together, but on a foundation of glass. I get the feeling that we're on borrowed time and it won't be long before everything shatters beneath our feet.

I've just walked in the door from a long day of work and giving samples for that damn paternity test. I want nothing more than a hot shower and a cold beer.

Beth is sitting on the couch with her back to me, watching some cooking show. I set my thermos of water down and she startles.

"Hey! I didn't even hear you come in. You've got to watch this. They're doing a barbecue contest. People from all over the world come set up in a parking lot to compete."

I walk over and sit down next to her. Her long hair is down and she's already washed the makeup off of her face. I note the fact that she's "borrowed" yet another of my t-shirts—something she seems to be doing daily now.

She doesn't break eye contact with the screen, "Doesn't it look delicious?"

I can't take my eyes off of her, "Yeah."

She turns to me, "You're not even looking at the television."

I smile, "I know. I saw something better that I'd like to eat."

The blush instantly creeps up her neck and face as she looks away. I've tried to keep myself in check since moving back in. Alan didn't feel that either of us was quite ready to jump back in with both feet. I admit that I didn't agree with him, but I want her forever this time. I don't want anything coming between us again. Watching her react to me like she does makes me second guess that decision though.

I'm going to need a cold shower.

Not like I haven't taken about a thousand of those recently.

I've got an idea though that I wanna run by her. "Beth, what if I took you to Galveston this weekend? We could see my mom...just get away from it all, yeah?"

She blinks as if she's still trying to clear her head from my previous comment and it takes everything in me to keep my face blank.

"Like where we got married?"

I place my hand on her knee and run my thumb lightly across her skin, the room is crackling with the electricity between us.

"Yeah, thought it might be good for us." *And I secretly hope that once we're there, you see how perfect we are together and call off the divorce.*

She smiles so big her eyes crinkle, "I'd love that. When can we leave?"

I kiss her forehead, "How about Friday morning?"

She agrees and my heart could burst with everything I feel for her. I'm going to need some ice cubes to add to my cold shower. My attraction to her was increasing with every day, so why did I continue to feel that it wouldn't last?

CHAPTER
TWENTY-FIVE
Beth

I can't believe we're doing this. We are taking a road trip to the place that could potentially hold even more memories for me, the place where I became Elizabeth Greene. It'll also be the place where I tell him that he's going to be a father...again (possibly).

What if he runs?

I mean, the man could potentially be the father of two kids soon. That's the kind of news you get right before you go to the store for milk, only to never be seen or heard from again.

I close my eyes and rest my head against the window of his truck, the sunlight beating through onto my face. I wonder how different our lives would be right now if we'd just kept our vows to each other.

David's voice pulls me from my thoughts, "You comfortable?" He gestures to the thermostat.

I nod, "I'm good. Um...I do need to pee again though."

He laughs, "Again? Has your bladder always been this small or do I have memory loss now?"

I chuckle nervously. We've had to stop every couple of hours since we got on the road at six this morning. I can't help it that this baby insists upon tap dancing on my bladder.

"Sorry. I drank a lot of water."

He laughs and taps the navigation screen to look for a nearby gas station. I pull my empire waist dress away from my body in an effort to hide the little bump that seems to be hell bent on making its presence known.

David finds a gas station to refuel at while I relieve my bladder and purchase more snacks. If anything, he'll probably attribute the belly bump to my recent eating habits. I found that eating often helped a lot with the nausea that is somehow still hanging on.

We drive a couple more hours before reaching Louisa's house mid-afternoon. My eyes are barely staying open at this point, so she gives me a warm hug and sends me upstairs to rest in David's old room. I wrap myself up in the navy plaid comforter and fall easily into a deep sleep.

When I wake, I can tell that it's early evening by the way the sun is coming in through the bedroom window. I roll over and look at the clock—six thirty? I can't believe I slept that long. I stretch out my limbs and enjoy the moment until I hear a quiet knock at the door.

"Beth? Dear, are you doing okay?"

I prop myself up on a pillow just as she comes in. "I'm sorry to sleep so late—I guess my early morning caught up with me."

She smiles and her gaze drifts down to my stomach where my bump is out in full force. I quickly pull the comforter up, but not before she sees.

"I was a lot like that when I was carrying David. If I wasn't throwing up, I was sleeping. That may explain why he's an only child." She laughs warmly until she sees my look of shock.

"Louisa, it's not—you can't—he doesn't know." My eyes plead with her to understand what I'm asking here.

She climbs onto the full-sized bed next to me and takes me into her arms. "I know you two have had your problems, but I've seen the way you look at each other. It's not all that different from how my John looked at me. You'll figure it out, I just know it."

I start weeping openly at her words and she rocks me in her arms as though I'm a child. It's exactly what I've needed since discovering the truth. When I received condemnation from my own mother, I needed someone to help shoulder this burden. I try to compose myself in fear of David hearing me.

"Shhhh…let it all out, sweet girl. I sent David to the store so I'd have some time alone with you. I made sure to add a few items that are always impossible to find so he should be gone a while yet."

I smile up at her through my tears, "How did you know? About the pregnancy, I mean."

She cups her hand under my chin and looks right into my eyes, "I suspected when David told me you ended up in the hospital a while back. The minute I saw your face though, it confirmed everything. You've got this glow about you—I know people always say that, but it's true."

I wipe my eyes and hug her tightly, "I'm so scared to tell him. How much did he tell you about what happened?"

She sighs, "I know everything—including what Jess is now claiming. I don't want to believe it's true though. How could he have made a child with her when he's so over the moon for you?"

I start crying again and can't answer her question. It's too cruel to think about it. Why didn't we see how much we loved each other before it came to this?

She continues to cradle me in her arms, "This is my fault, Beth. I relied on David too much after John passed."

"No! That's not true."

She hushes me, "It is. I took him away from you. John was so worried about you two. He felt that David worked too much and he was concerned with how you were handling everything on your own. I knew that and I selfishly wanted him here. It's not right."

She chokes up and I grip her tighter in my arms, wanting to take her pain away. I try to think of the words I could say to try and fix the situation.

There aren't any.

We sit in silence, letting our pain mingle with the tears.

"Do you know what it is yet?"

She gestures to my belly.

"No, it was still a little too soon. I do have some pictures in the pocket of my purse. I'll grab them." I push the comforter back and climb out of bed. Louisa watches my every move, her eyes still bright with tears.

I pull them out of the hidden pocket in my purse and hand them over. Her hand goes to her mouth as she studies each one and more tears begin to fall.

"Beth, don't you think the profile looks—"

"Like David's?" I finish for her.

She nods and goes back to admiring them before looking over at me again, "Would it be okay to, I mean would you mind if…"

She trails off as she searches for the right words and I grab her hand, placing it firmly on my abdomen. She nods again as if to let me know that's what she was trying to communicate. She places the pictures back on the bed and adds her other hand to my stomach.

"What a precious gift this is, Beth." She continues to stare reverently.

I place my hands on top of hers, "You're not going to tell him are you?"

She breaks eye contact with the bump and looks up at me, "Never. You'll tell him when you're ready. And Beth? He is going to be thrilled."

I smile.

I hope you're right, Louisa. I hope you're right.

CHAPTER
TWENTY-SIX
David

I finally make it back to the house after hours spent in the grocery store. She had the most obscure things on that damn list and I spent most of my time trying to track down employees to help me.

I carry the bags into the kitchen where the two of them are looking through photo albums together.

"There's my two favorite girls." I set the bags down and go over to them. I give my mom a kiss on the cheek and surprise Beth when I lift her up into my arms. My lips connect with hers and it's the first time since I moved home that I've kissed her like this.

My mom playfully swats at my arm, "Oh you two need to get a room!" I know that secretly she loves it though. The problems in my marriage broke her heart just as much as mine.

"Mom, was it really necessary for you to have brown rice flour and arrowroot powder? What in the hell are you making?"

She smiles innocently, "I found a recipe for gluten free bread that I want to try."

I massage the back of my neck, paying extra attention to the fact that Beth is standing in front of me, shell-shocked by our kiss. Her eyes are homed in on my lips and I'm pretty damn proud of the effect I have on her.

My mom clears her throat and I tear my gaze away from Beth. "Mom, you don't have a gluten allergy. Why are you going to all this trouble?"

She rolls her eyes at me, "David, there are a lot of people at church who have dietary restrictions. I'm just accommodating them."

She goes back to putting up the groceries when I stop her.

"Mom, when are you cooking for the people at church?"

She turns her back to me and places the flour up in the cabinet, "You never know when there will be a church potluck and I want to be prepared."

I sigh, "So, you had me get all of these ingredients on the off-chance that the church has a potluck?"

She smiles, "Exactly. Now help me put all of this away. Beth, is there anything that sounds good to you for dinner?"

I look over at Beth and smile. She's got a hand still pressed to her mouth and she jumps when my mom says her name.

"Sorry! I got lost in thought over here. Um, would it be awful if I said pizza sounds amazing right now?"

My mom chimes in, "Pizza sounds fabulous. We can order one in and make a salad to go with it."

I hold my hands up, "Why did I need to go to the store then?"

Beth and my mom exchange a look and start laughing. It's a damn good thing I love them as much as I do.

I wake when the sky begins to lighten. This old bed of mine is nothing like our king back home, but it definitely has its perks.

Beth is nestled in my arms, her breathing deep and even, and I find that this is the perfect opportunity to study her beautiful features.

Her blonde hair is lying across her face and I gently brush the strands back, before pressing my lips to her temple.

I know I shouldn't, but I pull the sheets back away from her body, needing to see all of her. She's wearing nothing more than a tank top and a pair of black cotton shorts and her nipples harden once the air conditioning kicks on. Her body seems different than I remember even from just a month ago, she's curvier. The stomach that seemed concave before, is now slightly rounded and I find that it makes me happy.

She lost so much weight right after everything, maybe this is a sign that she's content again. I place my hand on her lower abdomen and immediately pull it back. Where I expected her to be soft, she's not. Her body feels firm beneath my hand.

I place my hand back and begin gently moving it back and forth while my brain scrambles to come up with an answer.

Her breasts are bigger.

She is constantly taking naps.

She's been throwing up a lot.

No.

I do the math in my head and then when that doesn't give me a clear answer, I slide out of bed and grab my phone.

I sit in the floor and type in, "due date calculator." My screen fills with results and I click on one at random.

Date of last menstrual cycle

Yeah, I have no idea. I scroll down a little further.

Date of conception

I pinch the bridge of my nose while I try to remember the exact date. After narrowing it down, I type in June sixteenth. My heart is like a jackhammer in my chest.

The screen changes to confetti falling around a sign that reads:

Congratulations! Your baby is due March 9, 2015.

According to this, she's about to be fifteen weeks along. Beth stirs in bed and I damn near drop the phone when she mumbles my name. I freeze until I realize she's still asleep. I look back down at the screen.

Our baby is four inches long and weighs two and a half ounces. *Our baby.*

It's only the size of an apple. I don't need a pregnancy test to confirm what I already know.

Beth is pregnant.

She's pregnant with my baby, but didn't tell me.

I think back to that doctor's appointment I went to with Jess. I asked her if she was pregnant and she told me no.

I grab a pair of sweats and quietly pull them on before heading downstairs. It looks like I'm the only one up, which is perfect for what I'm about to do. I step out onto the patio and look up Beth's doctor. I know it's Saturday, but maybe someone will be there. A call center nurse answers on the third ring. "Good Morning, this is Cynthia."

I clear my throat, "Good Morning, Cynthia, this is David Greene. My wife, Elizabeth, is a patient of Dr. Harper's and she is having a lot of trouble with um…"

Think, David, think

"She's having trouble with throwing up still. Is that normal?"

"What is her date of birth?"

"December 5, 1983."

"And Mr. Greene, how far along is she?"

I swallow, "I think fourteen weeks. Is there any way I could get Dr. Harper to call me? We're out of town and I just want to make sure I don't need to take her in to a hospital."

"Yes sir, I can page her. What is a good number for you?"

I give her my number and then pace the patio, waiting for the call that will give me all the confirmation I need. I sink into a patio chair that is damp with dew, my head in my hands.

Please don't let Jess's baby be mine...

Please let Beth be pregnant.

I don't know if I'm praying or wishing at this point. All I know is that I feel like a bow string, pulled taut and ready to snap.

I jump when I hear the sliding door open and I guiltily stumble out of the chair.

Beth opens the door and then steps back inside to grab something. She comes back out carrying two cups of hot tea and I'm overtaken by a memory.

Beth comes into the kitchen and immediately wrinkles her nose. "What is that smell? It smells like something is burning."

She sniffs the air and I hold up her coffee. "I got you coffee. Is that what you're smelling?"

She looks at the cup like it contains poison and begins gagging. I'm still trying to process what the hell is wrong with her when she calmly walks over to the sink and vomits.

She hands me a cup and then sits in the chair opposite me. "Morning. I woke up when I realized you weren't in bed anymore. How long have you been up?" Her smile is still sleepy and I feel like an ass.

"I couldn't sleep so I thought I'd sit out here and enjoy the morning."

She takes in the humidity and grey skies before quirking a brow at me, "Really?"

I take a sip of the tea to avoid answering her, scalding my tongue in the process, before nodding vigorously.

She laughs at me, "It's hot. I would've warned you, but I thought the steam coming off the top would be enough. You sure you're okay?"

I set my tea down, "I'm fine—you still not drinking coffee?"

She shakes her head, "I'm kind of on a tea kick right now."

I reach my arms out to her, "C'mere."

She grins and sets her tea on the patio table before climbing into my lap and laying her head on my chest. I hope she can't feel how fast my heart is beating or she'll worry I'm about to have a heart attack.

She's sitting sideways which makes it easier. I bring my hand up and rest it on her stomach.

Her entire body stiffens and I see fear in her eyes. If I didn't know, I doubt I would've noticed the change, but it's definitely there.

I want to shout to the entire neighborhood that my wife is pregnant, but I want her to be the one to tell me. I can't force this or she'll run.

My phone rings in my pocket and I try to stand quickly without dumping her onto the patio. "I need to take this. It's about a job."

"Okay—you're working this weekend?"

I kiss her cheek before moving toward the front yard, "I'll be quick—I promise. Then I'm all yours."

She blows me a kiss and sits back down.

"Hello?"

"Hello, this is Dr. Harper. Is this David Greene?"

I unlock my truck and climb in. "Yes, it is. I called about Beth."

"I had to double check her records to make sure, but she does have you listed. What seems to be going on with her?"

"She's still throwing up. Is that normal?"

I'm holding my breath, waiting for her next words.

"Hmm…well she's about to be fifteen weeks so that should be subsiding soon. Is it like the episode before where she had to be hospitalized?"

I can no longer feel my arms.

She's pregnant.

My wife is pregnant.

In the midst of the chaos, we created life.

I hastily wipe at my eyes as tears form.

"Mr. Greene?"

"I'm sorry. No, it's not like before." *When I thought she had alcohol poisoning.* Was she even drinking that night?

"Make sure she keeps hydrating and if it worsens, it might not hurt to take her in to be evaluated. If that happens, page me again and I'll see what I can do from here."

I thank her and hang up. I rest my head on the steering wheel and laugh as tears fall.

I'm going to be a daddy.

CHAPTER
TWENTY-SEVEN
Beth

Louisa and I sit and enjoy our tea on the patio when David comes back. He looks upset and I immediately go to him.

"What happened? Are you okay?"

He starts laughing and it takes him a minute to catch his breath.

He's scaring me

David swings me around in his arms. "Beth, I'm better than fine. Just got the best news on a job that I've wanted for longer than I can remember."

I laugh, getting swept up in his euphoria, as Louisa eyes us both over a cup of coffee. "Tell us about this job, David."

He gives both of us a smug grin, "Well, there was one other guy bidding, but I got in there first and my bid was accepted. It's mine now and I'll be damned if I let it slip through my fingers."

Louisa and I congratulate him before I jump in, "This is the most excited I've ever seen you over a job. It must be good."

He wraps his arms around my waist again and his eyes look misty, "It was definitely a job worth waiting for and I'm going to prove that I'm the only man that can handle it—no matter what it takes."

Without waiting for a response, he leans down and kisses me soundly on the lips, effectively stopping my train of thought.

How odd

"I wanna take you to the beach today. Sounds good, yeah?"

FORSAKING ALL OTHERS

I nod stupidly, still trying to wrap my head around his excitement over another construction job.

"Go get packed and we'll head to Galveston."

I doze as we make the ninety minute drive to the ferry, the sky spitting rain onto the truck. Louisa backed out of going, saying she had to meet a friend for lunch. I think she wanted us to have this time alone though.

When I open my eyes, we're waiting in line for the ferry. We sit in lane five while country music plays softly on the radio. I turn from the window to find David staring at me.

"What? Did I drool on myself?"

He laughs and shakes his head, "You're beautiful—you know that?"

I smile, "I'm glad you think so, Mr. Greene."

He reaches for my hand, "I know so, Mrs. Greene."

We drive onto the ferry and park before heading to the front. The majority of the other passengers head to the upper viewing decks, but I've always liked being close to the water. I smile at the memory.

The air tastes of salt, something you can only experience on the ocean and I'm reminded of a Modest Mouse song. The ocean breathes salty indeed. I expected to see more people on the deck, but it's relatively quiet for a Saturday.

"Looks like we missed the summer crowd."

David agrees, "Yeah, it usually settles down after August—everyone's back in school by now."

I stand at the railing, letting the wind off the ocean whip my hair around. It's invigorating and I close my eyes, taking it all in.

David comes up behind me, threading his arms around my waist and resting his chin on my head. His hands make lazy circles across my stomach and my body stills.

It's the second time today that he's done it. The touch isn't unwanted—I find I can pretend that we're just a normal married couple, expecting our first child. That's all it is though—just pretend.

Does he know?

That thought leaves me with the urge to bring up the past and push him away, but I shove the thought back down and allow myself to enjoy him. I place my hands over his, holding him against me and he kisses the top of my head in response.

"Look at that!" My eyes open and David takes a hand off of me to point out into the ocean. "Dolphins."

I lean into the railing, searching the choppy water. Just when I think that I've missed them, two surface and gracefully dive back under. The sky brightens and the clouds begin to move away.

We may get a nice day at the beach after all.

I'll hold onto this memory forever and when things seem bad, I'll remember the feel of the ocean air, the dolphins, and my husband's arms cradling me and our baby.

CHAPTER
TWENTY-EIGHT
David

I'm mesmerized by my wife. Now that I know she's carrying my baby, I feel like I notice every detail. When she doesn't think I'm looking, she pats her abdomen as if she's reassuring our little one that everything's okay.

It's fucking adorable and I have to fight back tears of happiness.

She's mine forever now.

I packed some chicken salad sandwiches and chips for both of us—my mom actually gave me the idea—and we have a little picnic down on the beach. I checked online to make sure chicken salad was okay for her to eat while pregnant too.

Beth takes a ponytail holder from her wrist and pulls her hair back off of her face, all while laughing at some story I'm telling. She gives me her full attention as if every word I say is important. I wonder if she's always that focused on me.

After we eat, she kicks off her flip flops and wades out into the surf in her shorts.

"You sure that's safe?" I call out the warning before realizing my mistake.

She wrinkles her nose, "Why wouldn't it be safe?"

I laugh in an attempt to cover, "What are you going to wear to dinner if you get your clothes all wet?"

Smooth.

I mentally high-five myself.

She walks back over, the sand turning her feet golden brown. "Is there a place to change into my suit?"

I gesture over to a port-a-potty, "Not really. Aren't you wearing your suit under your clothes?"

She nods, "Yeah, but I brought a cover up."

Ah. She's afraid I'll see her stomach.

"What if I hold up the blanket and you can just change behind it?"

She bites her lower lip, "Yeah—that would work."

I clear our lunch stuff away and hold the blanket up. She doesn't have to know that I peeked once or twice.

I take her purse and our picnic leftovers and lock them in the truck before following her out into the water. I love this time of year. Mike and I spent nearly every weekend here as teens. The beaches aren't crowded and the water is still warm. The only drawback is that it's the start of hurricane season.

Out of habit, I scan the sky, checking for developing storms. The clouds have burned off and it's nothing but blue skies all around.

Beth hits a drop off and disappears under the water. I wade over and quickly pull her back up. She sputters and coughs as I bring her back to shallow water.

"I didn't see that coming!"

Her cover up is now plastered to her body like a second skin and I can fully appreciate her form. Her breasts are about to spill out of the black bikini top she's in and I silently give thanks. Her belly is small, but has a definite roundness to it. I would've missed it if I hadn't connected the dots early this morning.

I try to adjust myself discreetly in my suddenly tight swim

trunks, but Beth catches my eye and smiles.

Without a word, I take her hand and we wade out until the water is chest deep. I pull her body into mine, her legs wrapping around my waist.

She looks up at me and for the first time in what feels like an eternity, I see it in her eyes.

Trust.

I place my lips on her forehead, anchoring myself to her, before the current of emotions drags me out to sea.

I lift her up as the waves come rolling in and her hands grip my shoulders tightly.

"You wanna go back to shore?"

Her eyes glisten, "I just want you. Only you."

My heart plays out a steady beat before she pulls me down to her mouth, one hand looped around my shoulder while the other is tangled in my hair.

I press her body closer to mine, the water lapping around us. Beth lowers her hand and places it on the waistband of my shorts, and I bite back a groan.

The ocean is teeming with bacteria

Where the hell did that thought come from?

I grab her hand, "We can't—it's not safe."

She gives me a panicked look, "Is there a shark?"

I laugh and bring us closer to the shoreline, "No sharks. When I take you, it won't be in an ocean full of God knows what."

She lowers herself until her feet touch the sand, the water now only waist deep, "Does this mean you're finally giving in?"

I laugh, "Yeah, you've worn me down." I look at where the sun is in the sky, "but first—dinner."

She stands on her tiptoes and nips at my bottom lip with her teeth, "You sure about that?"

Lust has clouded my thoughts and if it weren't for the baby, I'd probably be giving in right now.

I adjust my shorts before wading to shore, "Yeah...dinner."

"That was really good," Beth sleepily whispers against my chest. We're sitting on the ferry and all I can think about is how fast I can drive to get us back to my mom's house.

Once I pulled Beth from the ocean and back onto solid ground, we walked along the shoreline until we came to the spot where she took my last name.

I thought I'd have to remind her, but she immediately stopped and looked around. It's nothing more than a simple wooden arbor that has somehow been able to withstand years of hurricanes. The symbolism isn't lost on me.

"Here—we got married here, didn't we?"

"We did." I cleared my throat as my voice began to waver.

She took a piece of old beach wood and carved our initials in the sand. Once she finished, I took the wood from her and carved "Always" underneath it. She teared up at the *Harry Potter* reference.

I never thought anything would top our wedding day, but this—this day spent with her may just surpass it.

We had dinner at *Gaido's* and I'm sure the food was delicious, but I was a little too preoccupied to enjoy it.

I pull her in closer to me and answer, "It was the best, babe."

I hope she knows I'm not talking about the food.

CHAPTER TWENTY-NINE
David

We pull up outside my mom's house a little after ten. Beth fell asleep once we left the ferry and hasn't moved once. I shut the truck off and carry her inside.

She stirs a little when I place her on the bed, but then settles right back into a deep sleep.

She's not waking up again tonight.

The thought makes me inwardly groan. I've been uncomfortable since we stepped out of the ocean, what's another eight hours or so?

I walk into the en suite bathroom and start the water.

Looks like it's another cold shower for me.

I've just stepped under the freezing showerhead when I feel the curtain move. I open my eyes and there she is.

I blink several times, not entirely convinced I didn't fall asleep and dream her.

"Can I join you?" Her words are weighted and she grins wickedly at me.

I nod dumbly, all the blood has left my brain at this point.

The cold spray of water hits her body and she sucks in a breath, "C-c-could we warm it up a bit there, David? That's awful."

I need a minute to fully take in her body. "I don't know. I kinda like the effect it has on you, baby."

Beth crosses her arms over her chest and gives me a stern look.

I laugh and turn the handle over to hot, the water instantly warming us both. "Do you make a habit of spying on people in the shower?"

She blushes before dropping her arms away from her body, "I thought we could finish what we started earlier. You look like you're up for it."

I follow her gaze down and bite my lip. I want nothing more than to launch myself at her right now, but I need to take it slow.

"C'mere." I hold out my hand and she obliges. Pregnancy has only enhanced her beauty, making me crave her even more. "Jesus, Beth. Your—" I gesture at her chest, suddenly unable to form a complete sentence.

"Tits?" she supplies helpfully.

I nod slowly, "Fucking amazing, babe." I lower my mouth to one and she rewards me with a moan that echoes off the shower tiles.

"You taste like the ocean," I whisper against her skin.

She doesn't speak, just reaches down and grips me in her hands. When she uses her tongue along the tattoo of her name, all rational thought ceases.

"Mmm…your skin is salty." She murmurs the words and I damn near come undone.

I twist her hair around my hand and gently pull her mouth back up to mine. My other hand is gripping her hip and my thumb is perfectly aligned with her belly. I lightly skim it up and down and love that she doesn't try to stop me.

When she sucks my bottom lip into her mouth, I free my hand from her hair and bring it between her legs.

"You're soaked, babe."

Her eyes flutter open briefly, "Just for you."

I growl and use my fingers to bring her right to the edge. Her breathing quickens and I know she's close. I stop at the last second and pull my fingers from her warm body.

Her eyes fly open, "W-w-why did you s-stop?"

"Say it. Say you'll call off the divorce...please." My words surprise me, I don't beg—but I need to hear it. I want to know this isn't goodbye for her.

I expect her to argue, but she doesn't, "I don't want a divorce. I can't imagine my life without you in it. Please..." Her eyes plead with me to finish what I started.

I kiss her soundly on the mouth, my tongue joining with hers. "I love you, Beth Greene."

I lower my hand back down and give in to her pleas. Her moans turn to quiet screams and then she goes limp. Before she's fully recovered, I shut off the shower and lift her into my arms.

The cool air makes the hair on her arms stand up so I lay her gently on the bed and cover her body with mine. I want to take it slow and enjoy every moment, but I've waited too long for this.

I push myself into her body and groan at how tight she is. It's like coming home and my thrusts increase as her nails run down my back.

"David...don't stop. Don't stop. I'm close..." Her voice trails off with a cry and she comes undone.

I watch the look on her face thanks to the bathroom light streaming in and follow her over the edge, her name on my lips.

It's only after I've gotten her a towel so that she can dry herself off that I realize I wasn't gentle with her.

"Are you okay? You feel okay?"

She lays back against the pillows, her eyes closed and a smile on her face, "I'm fantastic, David. How about you?"

I worriedly scan her body, "I'm fine—you don't hurt

anywhere? I didn't hurt you?"

She laughs, "David, I'm good. Why are you worrying? You know I'm not made of glass."

I climb into bed next to her, "I got a little carried away."

She nestles in closer to me, her back to my chest, "I like it when you get carried away. You should do it more often."

I place my hand on her abdomen and fall asleep almost immediately.

CHAPTER THIRTY
Beth

I wake with a stretch in an empty bed. Thoughts from the night before flood in and I grin to myself. I missed him…so much. Tears flood my eyes and now I'm crying. These hormones have me all mixed up and turned upside down.

As we walked along the beach yesterday, my mind screamed, *Tell him! Tell him you're pregnant!*

I wanted to do just that, but the timing was all wrong. Once he drew *Always* in the sand, I actually opened my mouth to shout it out, but he interrupted me and insisted that I eat. After stuffing myself on flounder, crab cakes, and crème brûlée—I was worthless. My eyes grew heavy and I dozed on the ferry ride. Once we got into the truck, I rested my head against the window and fell into a deep, dreamless sleep.

I woke in his bed and heard the shower running not long after we got home. *Now or never.* I meant what I told him. I should've called off the divorce long before now. It wasn't fair to him. I just had myself convinced that he was the father of Jess's baby and I talked myself out of a life with him. I have to think like Louisa in this situation or I'll end up slowly driving myself insane.

There's a light knock at the door and David walks into the bedroom, carrying a cup of hot tea. He hands it to me and sits down on the edge of the bed.

"You sleep okay?" He gives me a sly smile that I can't help but return.

"I did. How about you?"

He cracks his neck, "I slept like a rock. Is there uh any way you'd be up for round two?"

My pulse picks up while my inner romantic is stripping off clothes and racing toward the bedroom.

My voice sounds husky, "I'm game if you are."

He exhales slowly, "Damn. Will the wanting you ever go away?"

I smile up at him, "I sure hope not."

He stands up quickly and strips down to nothing and I have to set my hot tea down before I scald myself. He pulls back the comforter, I think he's expecting me to be dressed. I never bothered putting anything back on last night and by the look on his face, he's enjoying the view.

He doesn't waste any time before he's pushing himself inside me and all I seem to be capable of doing is holding onto him and making unintelligible sounds.

His thrusts push me over the edge and I press a hand to my mouth to quiet my screams.

David speaks through clenched teeth, "Be as loud as you want. My mom isn't home."

I drop my hand and cry out his name.

He wraps my hair in his hand and bruises my lips with his mouth. It's not long before the second orgasm overtakes me and it's even more intense than the first. *Thank you, pregnancy hormones.*

David tugs my hair back until it borders on painful, leaving my throat bared to him. He runs kisses up and down my neck and then with a growl, fills me.

FORSAKING ALL OTHERS

I come down from my high.

He didn't use protection.

Not that it matters really, but he's always so careful.

He feathers kisses across my throat and looks up at me lazily. "I don't think I said it before, but good morning."

I laugh in spite of my thoughts, "It has definitely been a good morning."

We spend the rest of the day walking around town and letting Louisa spoil us with her cooking. I can't think of a time where I've had more fun.

I wake up Monday morning, wrapped in two hundred pounds of alpha male, and ready to enjoy our last day here.

I sit up just enough to see the clock, it's almost nine o'clock. I slide back down onto the pillow and smile to myself.

Best vacation ever.

I feel him stir behind me and his hand seeks out my bump before he relaxes. I cover his hand with mine.

Today is the day.

No more secrets. Come what may—I'm going to tell him. I just need to be brave.

"Mornin' baby, did you sleep well?" He murmurs the words into my hair and I love that it gives me shivers.

I roll to face him, cupping his face in my hands. "I'm sleeping better than I knew was possible, thanks to you."

His beard tickles my face as he presses his lips to mine, "Care to join me in the shower?"

I grin, "Might this invitation have anything to do with what is pressed up against my hip right now?"

I move my hand down and he tries to stifle a groan. I'm sure Louisa will enjoy sleeping in a quiet house again. As if reading my thoughts, David tilts my chin up, "Farmer's market—said she'd be there until ten thirty—said we needed more alone time last night."

"Having trouble with your words, baby?" I work my hand a little faster and his head falls back. I like watching the reactions I can draw out of him. It makes me feel powerful to have this control over him.

"Beth...don't stop."

His phone starts buzzing on the nightstand and I stop. He barely gets the words out this time, "Don't. Stop. Please."

I can tell he's close, so I block out the sound of his cellphone vibrating and send him over the edge, his fists have the sheets in a death grip.

The vibrating starts back up again when he goes to start the shower.

"David? It's ringing again. Do you want me to—?"

He storms out of the bathroom, "If this is one of my guys, he's gonna wish he would've listened to me when I said not to bother me."

He looks at the screen and answers, "Hello? This is he... That was fast...How do I get that? No, I'm out of town for another day...Could you fax it? Yeah? Let me get you the number..."

He walks out of the bedroom and over to the upstairs office. I take a minute to relieve my bladder while waiting for him to come back. I check the water temperature in the shower and find it's just now lukewarm, so I brush my teeth and check out my reflection.

I've got dark circles from the mascara under my eyes and my hair is hopeless, but I've never been happier. I jump in fright when

I see David's reflection in the mirror. He looks as if his phone call didn't end well.

"You okay?"

He nods and wraps his arms around me, "Shower with me?"

"Of course, let me just grab some clothes to wear after."

He turns me around until I'm facing him and kisses me fiercely. He kisses me like he's never going to get the opportunity to do it again before breaking free and stepping into the shower.

I walk out of the bathroom and grab a sundress when I hear the fax machine down the hall. I know I shouldn't pry, but I want to see whatever it is that's made him so upset. Hopefully, it's not the job he just worked so hard to get.

I walk silently down the carpeted hallway and into the office. There are three papers sitting on the machine and I snatch them up before I can change my mind.

My eyes skim over it and I discover why he kissed me like he did just mere seconds ago. He was kissing me goodbye.

The alleged father, DAVID GREENE, cannot be excluded as the biological father of the fetus as they share genetic markers. Using the above system, the probability of paternity is 99.99%...based upon the samples submitted from the mother, JESSICA DAVIS, and the DNA extracted from the population of fetal cells.

Presence of Y chromosome—indicates that fetus is male

They're having a son.

I suck air into my lungs, my vision blurring. I'm about three seconds away from a panic attack.

I need to leave

I can't stay here

I stifle a sob and begin hurriedly packing my things. It doesn't matter that I pictured this happening a thousand times, I never imagined that it would hurt this badly.

CHAPTER THIRTY-ONE
David

I'm under the showerhead for about ten minutes when I realize she hasn't joined me yet. To be fair, I would've noticed a hell of a lot sooner had I not just gotten the phone call I did.

The lab had a rush on the orders, so they wanted to let me know as soon as possible. I feel like the world I just built this weekend is about to implode.

Two kids...

The thought makes me feel sick. I'm going to subject Beth to being around Jess indefinitely. She'll be in our lives for birthdays and holidays every fucking year from here on out.

I slam my fist into the tile in frustration. It's so unfair—when Beth and I were so close to reconciliation. I feel like this weekend with her was a glimpse into what our lives could've been like and now that's been snatched out from under us.

I get out and wrap a towel around my waist. I'm going to have to sit her down and tell her. I just pray that she stays put. Hell, who am I kidding? She's going to bolt the first chance she gets.

"Beth?"

I look around the bedroom—empty.

"Baby? Where are you?"

I walk down the hall and see the papers from the fax machine, lying on the desk, and I know that she's gone.

I walk back into the bedroom and see that her purse and

suitcase are gone as well.

"Fuck!" I roar at the empty room.

"David? What's wrong?" My mom comes running up the stairs. Looks like she came home early.

I sink down onto the side of the bed, my head in my hands. "She's gone. She's gone and it's my fucking fault!"

I hand her the papers and she reads over them quickly before making a sound of protest, "No—Oh my God—David!" I halfway expect her to hit me upside the head like she did when I screwed up as a kid. She surprises me with a rough hug, her tears falling onto my head.

She lets me go long enough to wipe her streaming eyes, "Where is she, David? Where's Beth?"

I stare at a blank spot on the wall in front of me, "I don't know. Was my truck here when you got back?"

She goes over to the window and looks out, "Your truck is still here."

My cell phone starts vibrating again and it takes me a second to locate it on the dresser.

Lauren.

I put the phone on speaker.

"Laur—where is she? Is she okay?" I'm practically shouting the words.

Her voice sounds distressed, "Dave, she's in a cab on her way to the airport in Houston. I'm trying to get her on a flight home. What happened? She didn't make any sense when she called."

I sigh and fight back tears, "She left, Laur. They faxed over the paternity test results and the baby's mine. I'm having a son with Jess."

I can hear Lauren repeating everything to someone in the

background, probably Mike. "Lauren, is that Mike?"

She comes back on the line, "Yeah, David—he brought me breakfast at work. I need you to listen to me. Elizabeth is pregnant and—"

I interrupt her, "I know she is. That's why it makes this so much worse!"

She goes silent, then quietly asks, "She told you?"

I shake my head, "I think she was getting close to telling me, but I figured it out on my own a few days ago."

Lauren says something else to Mike. "Dave, I don't know if Elizabeth told you, but we ran into Jess at a doctor's appointment last Monday. It was the same day that she took the paternity test—I overheard her talking with a nurse and something sounded off. I just have a gut feeling that Jess tampered with those test results, but I'm going to need some time to prove it."

I pinch the bridge of my nose and close my eyes, my mom's hand squeezing mine tightly. "How do you suggest I do that? We're supposed to go before the judge next week. I'm pretty sure she won't call off the divorce now."

Mike says something to Lauren, but I can't make it out. Lauren laughs, "That's it! David, Mike just found something that could be your saving grace. You're going to need to get your ass back here and file a motion with the court for an emergency hearing—"

I stop her, "You want me to rush back to town and push up my divorce? How is that going to help?"

"David—listen to me. In the state of Texas, if a woman is pregnant, the judge cannot grant a divorce. All you have to do is request a pregnancy test in the hearing. That will give me the time I need to get proof. Okay?"

My fist comes up to my mouth, I'm doing my damnedest to

hold these emotions in check, "Lauren, I think you just gave me my Christmas gift early. Thank you so much!"

She laughs, "Don't thank me yet, I've still got to prove that Jess tampered with the paternity test. Also, Elizabeth could still file for divorce, but the baby would have to be born before they would allow it."

"You worry about the test and I'll take care of Beth's desire to leave. Don't book any flights—I'm going to get her."

We hang up and I look over at my mom, who is a blubbering mess. "Mom—I'm gonna have to cut this visit short, but as soon as this gets sorted, I'm bringing my wife back here."

She blinks away tears, "How did you know she was pregnant?"

I pause, "You knew?"

She sniffles and nods, "I suspected she might be when you had to take her to the hospital a month or so ago. I knew she was when I saw that sweet little baby belly and the way she just had this glow about her."

I nod, "I knew when I finally saw her stomach and I called her doctor's office to verify. I had a hunch she'd have me as an authorized party on the account—turns out that hunch paid off."

She pats me on the back and pulls me into a hug, "Go get her, David. And don't ever let her go."

I give her a quick kiss on the cheek.

I was getting my wife back—if I had to drag her kicking and screaming from that airport.

CHAPTER
THIRTY-TWO
Beth

Do you know how much a taxi from Beaumont to Houston costs? A little over two hundred dollars and one emergency credit card later, I'm sitting in the airport waiting on Lauren to find me a flight.

Me:

Any luck? I'm here.

Lauren:

**Well, there are a lot of people flying here today.
I'll keep trying.**

Me:

Okay.

I tear up again and that familiar tightening in my chest becomes more noticeable. I already scared the poor cab driver with my hysterical sobbing, I really don't want to lose control in a crowded airport. They might not let me on a flight.

I lean over and hug my knees, focusing on the patterned tiles.

Deep breaths

In and out

I give up and pull some medication from my purse—I can't

even remember the last time I needed it. I'm about to pop one when I read the label: *Consult with a physician if you are pregnant or nursing.*

I sigh, putting everything back in my purse. *Guess it's back to knee hugging and deep breathing.*

I close my eyes and try to visualize something peaceful, but all I can think of is David.

When I open them again, there are a pair of familiar work boots standing directly in front of me.

I look up and there he is. It's as if I conjured him with my mind. "What are you doing here?"

He kneels down, "Did you really think I'd leave you behind, Beth?"

I bite my lip as my eyes well up again, looking anywhere but at him when I answer. "I don't know. I figured after you got the results, you'd be leaving soon. I couldn't bear the thought of you with her, so I ran. It's the only thing I seem to be good at doing!"

"What about growing our baby in the middle of absolute chaos? You seem to be doing a phenomenal job there."

My head jolts up, "You know? Did Lauren or your mom tell you?"

He laughs, "Baby, you've thrown up more in the last month than in the entire time I've known you, you're more emotional, and you have the sexiest baby bump I've ever seen—I put all the pieces together this weekend."

My mouth is dry, "You-you're not mad?"

He reaches out and rests his hands on my knees, "No, I wish you would've told me when I ran into you at that doctor's appointment back in August, but I get why you didn't. None of that matters anymore, because you're mine forever now."

"What about Jess? And the results?"

He gives me a sad smile, "I don't know, Beth. Lauren seems to think it might be fraudulent based on a conversation she overheard between Jess and a nurse."

I put my head back down in despair, "Forgery? David, it seems like a longshot. How is Lauren planning on proving this?"

He spins his wedding band around his finger, focusing on the floor, instead of me. "I don't know—I don't have a fucking clue how any of this works out!"

I glance around to make sure no one's heard him. The last thing I need is to end up on a "no-fly list."

I cock my head toward the sliding doors. "Let's discuss this outside, please."

He grabs my suitcase, "Let's discuss it in the truck, while we drive back home."

I shake my head, "Oh no you don't. I need to wrap my mind around all of this, David. I don't know if I can stomach sharing special events with Jess for the rest of our lives."

He grabs my hands, "You told me you were calling off the divorce. Are you telling me you've changed your mind?"

I focus on the arrivals/departures board in front of me, "I-I don't know. I said that before—before we knew for sure it was yours."

He laughs sardonically, "So, what was all that the other night then? More lies? Jesus Beth, can't you be honest with me about anything?"

I'm about to lay into him when a family of four walks past. Instead, I walk away from him and out into the humidity that is Houston.

David follows me, "Beth, I'm sorry. I shouldn't have snapped at you. I get that you're under a lot of stress and I'm not making this any easier on you. I just wanted you to choose a life with me, regardless of the test results, but that's not fair to you."

I suck in a ragged breath, I'm not sure if it's the humidity or panic attack that's causing me to feel like I'm breathing underwater. "David, I want a life with you—this weekend has been the best reminder of why we should be together. On the other hand, knowing that I would have to share you with Jess—who seems hell-bent on sticking her claws into you—it feels impossible. That, and I'm worried about what diseases you picked up while knocking her up." It's a cheap shot and I regret the words almost instantly.

He grabs onto my wrists so hard that I cry out in pain, "I have never been with anyone, but you without protection. Did I fuck up? Yes! Am I going to have to live the rest of my life knowing what I did to you? Yes!"

He growls the words through clenched teeth before letting me go abruptly and walking away. I think he's going to leave until he stops and leans his head against the building.

He's trying to keep himself in check.

I want to stay where I'm at and pout, but I know I've hurt him just as much as he's hurt me. I walk over to where he's standing, ignoring the curious looks of those around me. "David, I'm sorry. I shouldn't have said that. I wish there was some sort of guarantee you could give me that you're not the father."

He hastily wipes at his eyes and turns around to face me. *I made David Greene cry?*

"I can't give you that, baby. You're gonna have to choose me as is."

I swallow hard, a million thoughts racing through my head. I tune them out and finally answer him with my heart, "You, as is, is a hell of a lot better than not having you at all."

I'd wanted a fairy tale my entire life, but when given the chance, I'd take a harsh reality with no secrets over a night of dress up any day.

He holds his fist up to his bottom lip, "Are you saying what I think you're saying?"

I quit trying to reign in my emotions and let my tears flow freely, "I'm saying I want you to be my husband—" I run a hand along my baby bump, "—and the father to this little person, regardless of what that paternity test shows. I have to trust you on this...and I'm slowly learning to do just that."

David wraps me up in his big arms, showering my face with kisses, "I love you so much Elizabeth Marie Greene, and I will do everything in my power to prove it to you for the rest of our lives."

I slept most of the ride home, David's hand resting on my head. Whenever he stopped for gas, he would wake me for a bathroom break and to buy snacks—he seemed to think I constantly required food—something I wasn't correcting at the moment.

We arrive back to our house after dark and as we unpack, I finally ask the question that's been on my mind since we left the airport. "David, what would you have done if I would've refused to come with you?"

He places some clothes in the dresser and turns back to face me, "I would've thrown you over my shoulder and carried you out. I told you, you're mine forever."

I smile, "Yes, but what if I wasn't willing to call off the divorce?"

He laughs, "Beth, I would've done the same thing. Lauren and Mike gave me some interesting news this morning."

I give him a "go on" look, "I would've filed a motion for an emergency hearing, where I would've requested a pregnancy test," seeing my confusion, he continues, "Apparently in the great state of Texas, a judge cannot grant a divorce when the woman is pregnant. So, looks like you're stuck with me." His confidence wavers a bit toward the end and he actually seems unsure of himself.

I laugh incredulously, "Are you kidding me? So my plans to drug you in order to flee to the nearest courthouse are all for naught?"

His smile returns, "Would you have hated me for it?"

I bite my lip as I decide how to best answer him, "I've tried to hate you since that night, but I can't. You're like a poison in my bloodstream, and at the same time—my oxygen. I don't know how to be Beth without David."

He drops the clothes in his hands, "Fuck—I mean shoot. I did some research and at fifteen weeks, the baby can start to hear outside the womb. I've gotta clean up my language."

My eyes fill with tears, "You know how far along I am?"

David runs his hand over his beard and I can tell he's deciding how to answer me. "I did the math and I may or may not have called up Dr. Harper to confirm that."

I gasp, "The important job you got?—that was it wasn't it? Beating out the other guy because you got your bid in first?" I'm leaning over, wheezing with laughter now.

"Dam—darn it, Beth. I was so effing proud that you were carrying my baby, but I wanted you to tell me when you were ready." He tosses a pillow at me, "Stop laughing—it's not funny!"

I continue laughing until tears pour down my face, "I'm

sorry—I can't get over the fact that you compared getting me pregnant to getting the bid on your dream job. I thought you were awfully excited about it."

He comes over to me and wraps his arms around my waist, and drawls, "I'm torn between wanting to strip you down and get in there real nice and deep-like or treating you like you're made of glass and not touching you for the next twenty-five weeks."

I feel as if the air has been sucked from the bedroom and I answer breathlessly, "The first choice. Definitely the first one."

Then I throw caution to the wind and jump into his arms. He pulls my shirt up, placing a sound kiss on our baby, "Okay, twist my arm—but tomorrow, we're going down to the courthouse and withdrawing those divorce papers."

I quickly agree before reaching for the button on his jeans, "Whatever you say, Mr. Greene."

CHAPTER THIRTY-THREE

David

"So you wish to withdraw the petition for divorce?" The county clerk ignores me and focuses solely on Beth.

"Yes, that's correct."

The clerk spends the next few minutes looking up our file. "Here we go, Elizabeth Marie Greene and David Michael Greene. Looks like he never filed a response, so we'll just need you to fill out a form to dismiss everything."

I smile cockily, I can't help myself—I've been given everything I wanted. I don't even care.

Beth is busy signing the required documents when we hear a commotion near the front doors.

"Let me in. I have information the court must hear!"

I move until my body is shielding Beth's from whatever the hell is taking place near us. She puts down her pen and turns in confusion. "What's going on?"

I shake my head, "Not a clue—stay here." I make my way to the front doors and there's Lauren—in a stand-off with several other people.

"David!" She sounds out of breath, "Thank God! I was just about to call my boyfriend, *Detective Mike Sullivan*, to sort this out." She eyes one man suspiciously.

The whole thing is so ludicrous, it makes me laugh. "What seems to be the problem here?"

FORSAKING ALL OTHERS

The man getting the death glare from Lauren answers, "This woman barged into the courtroom and demanded to be heard. No one knew who she was or why she was there though."

I look over at Lauren, who is studying the ceiling intently. "Laur?—what the hell?"

She pants slightly from being out of breath, "Well, you were meant to be in the court making your grand stand. That's what I told you to do, so I assumed you listened. It would've been much more dramatic!"

I look at the man restraining her, "She's here for us."

He gives me a puzzled look, "You're sure? She seems kind of unhinged."

Lauren clears her throat, "I can hear you." She looks back at me, "Where's Elizabeth? She's going to want to hear this."

I thank the man and lead Lauren away from the crowd, "You could've gotten arrested pulling that shit. What the hell were you thinking?"

She smiles, "I thought it'd be like one of those courtroom dramas, where the key witness rushes in at the eleventh hour with information that could turn the case around."

I roll my eyes, "You watch too much television—you know that?"

She slaps my arm good-naturedly, "Let's get this show on the road, Dave!"

Beth is just finishing up when we arrive, "Lauren, what are you doing here?"

Lauren gestures to the chair, "You're going to want to sit down for this." She looks over at the clerk, "If you weren't already sitting down, I'd suggest you do so as well."

The clerk ignores her completely and goes about her

paperwork.

Lauren leans over, still trying to catch her breath. "Laur—you okay?" Beth pats her on the back.

"Yeah," she wheezes, "I may have run a bit farther than I'm used to. Just give me a sec—I've got a side cramp."

I sit in a chair and begin restlessly tapping my fingers along the armrest, "Sometime today, Lauren."

Her phone dings and her eyes brighten once she sees it, "Okay, our guest is walking in. We can begin."

She leaves and comes back with a woman I don't recognize. I look over at Beth and it's obvious she knows her.

"Rose?" Beth asks questioningly.

The woman, Rose, nods, "Hi Elizabeth."

Lauren interjects, "Okay, here we go—I did some digging after we hung up yesterday, David. I kept running into dead ends until I thought to go visit our new friend, Rose. Turns out, Rose had been doing some digging too. There were a lot of record inconsistencies with the chart of Jessica Davis. She's been seen regularly in the recent months, but never by a doctor on staff. There's only been one nurse to see her every single visit—"

I interrupt, "Carolyn?" It was the only nurse we ever saw.

Lauren nods, "Carolyn Brandon. Last week, I overheard Jess offering Carolyn money—I initially thought she was looking to have an abortion, but something didn't make sense."

I circle my hand, growing impatient, "Wrap it up, Lauren. What did you find out?"

Rose answers, "Jessica Davis is not pregnant, nor has she ever been."

I drop my hand weakly and Beth makes a small sound of surprise before asking, "But the paternity test?—how?"

FORSAKING ALL OTHERS

Rose continues, "I've gone back and reviewed everything. It appears that Carolyn was paid an unknown amount of money to disclose patient information and to forge the test results."

I look up, "If that sample for the paternity test didn't come from Jess, then who did it come from?"

Rose smiles and looks over at Beth, "The blood sample used in the paternity test came from your wife, Mr. Greene. The lab confirmed it this morning."

I stand up suddenly, "That means that—"

Beth gets up and walks toward me, tears flowing freely down her face, "That means that we're having a little boy!"

I pick her up in my arms and note that the clerk who wasn't interested in us a minute ago is now leaning over her desk, completely absorbed.

I look over at Rose, "So, what's going to happen now?"

"Well, besides there being a huge HIPAA violation—both women will be charged. Jessica will be hit with lesser charges of solicitation to tamper with medical records while Carolyn will be facing tampering charges along with falsifying medical records. Paternity fraud charges will most likely be added in as well. I think it's safe to say that you won't be bothered by either one of them anytime in the near future."

Lauren is grinning like a cat who just caught a canary, "Did I come through or what?"

I grab her arm and pull her into our impromptu group hug, "You did better than I could've imagined."

Rose smiles, "I've got to go, but Lauren has all of my contact information. Don't hesitate to call if you have any questions."

I look down at Beth, who is laughing and sobbing simultaneously. I kiss her on the lips, "We're having a little boy,

Beth."

She wraps her arms around my neck, "I feel like I'm dreaming right now."

I smile at her words.

I've felt like I was dreaming since she agreed to stay with me yesterday—even without knowing what today's outcome would be.

I feel like the luckiest son-of-a-bitch alive. I don't know it yet, but my luck's about to take a turn for the worse.

CHAPTER THIRTY-FOUR

December 5, 2014
(27 weeks)

"Happy birthday, baby." David's warm breath tickles my ear and I burrow back under the comforter.

I sleepily reply, "I'm not ready to be thirty-one though."

He strokes my much rounder belly, "That's too bad, because I booked a spa day for the birthday girl. If you see her, let me know."

I pull the covers back, "You did? When?"

David turns and looks back at the clock on his nightstand, "Your appointment is in an hour, so you might want to get moving."

I roll over to face him, "You're the best ever—you know that right?"

He kisses my nose, "Anything for my girl. Do you want some hot tea?"

I smile and little man begins kicking in my belly. I grab David's hand and place it back on my belly. "Your son is telling you good morning."

Like he's done ever since that first kick, David gets this mesmerized look on his face and begins talking to his son, "Hey little man. You working on your mornin' swim?"

And like I've done ever since that first kick, I tear up. I never thought we'd be here—in this place. I never imagined that we would be able to claw our way back to each other, but here we are.

I got to witness my tough guy of a husband cry at his first ultrasound appointment. It was funny, something that I'd become accustomed to, was a brand new world for him. He held my hands in a death grip and kept whispering, "We made that. That's our little man."

David interrupts my thoughts, "What about Lucas?"

I wrinkle my nose, "I don't know…I'm not feeling it."

It's the one thing we cannot agree on—baby names. I want to wait until March, when he's born, and see what he looks like. David wants it decided now so that he can finish up the nursery. Apparently, he's building a wooden sign with the baby's name— I've been forbidden from entering the workshop because he wants it to be a surprise.

"David, what if you just use our last name over his crib?" I know this is an exercise in futility here. He'll just keep trying to wear me down.

He scoffs, "I can't have a kid with no name, Beth. What about Michael?"

"Your middle name? I don't know…it's not great."

The only thing we've agreed on is the middle name—John, after his dad. It felt right, and with such an important middle name, I want to have the perfect first name to go with it. I guess if this is what we're fighting about now—we've come a long way.

David sighs and then smiles at me mischievously before sliding his hand between my legs, "What if we agree to disagree for the moment?"

I'm instantly wet—*seriously a good strong breeze in his presence just about does it for me these days*. I kind of thought the hormones would taper off, but if anything, they've increased.

FORSAKING ALL OTHERS

David had a long talk with Dr. Harper at our last check-up about it. That wasn't embarrassing or anything—nope, not one bit. He wanted to make sure that it was safe for the baby, first and foremost. Secondly, he wanted to know if it was normal for a pregnant woman to want sex every day—sometimes more than once. I mean that only happened on one occasion—two occasions, tops.

Dr. Harper mercifully was on my side and said as long as I felt okay and had no complications that we were okay to have sex up until the baby was born. She then told David that some of her patients end up on bedrest and are unable to have sex for a good chunk of their pregnancy. He didn't ask questions after that.

His hand slips beneath the waistband of my sweatpants, "You're awfully quiet over there. Was that a yes?"

I moan as his fingers stroke me, "Yes...always yes."

I pull into the driveway late that same afternoon. The sky is already darkening and it makes me miss the late evenings of summer. I pull my relaxed body from the warmth of my car. When David said "spa day," I envisioned a facial and maybe a massage, if I was lucky. No, he booked me an entire package of services. I got there and they started with an aromatherapy bath before a prenatal massage. I was served lunch on fine china before I was whisked away for a facial and then my day ended with a manicure and pedicure. Considering I haven't been able to reach my feet in the past few weeks, that may have been my favorite part.

I set my purse down on the kitchen counter and am in the process of debating whether or not to take a nap when the doorbell rings. I look through the peephole and see that it's Landon.

My blood runs cold. I haven't seen him in person in months—he's been a favorite for the local news stations as he tirelessly searches for Katya. I feel awful that the poor woman has been missing for four months now, and police still have no leads. Landon won't give up though—he even put her picture up on billboards.

My heart breaks for him, but I'm still wary of opening the door. I hear my garage door open and panic sets in before I realize it's David. I'm going to have to deal with this before he gets involved.

I take a deep breath and open the door.

"Hi Landon."

He stares at my face, I'm still fresh-faced from the spa, and he frowns. "Elizabeth? Are you sick?"

I smile, "No—just spent the day at the spa," I hear David walk in, and I know I need to wrap this up. "What can I do for you?"

Landon looks over my shoulder as David comes up behind me. He wraps his arms possessively around my waist, resting his hands on my belly. Landon's gaze travels downward and he actually stumbles back a step, "No…" his words are whispered, but I can read the look of anguish on his face.

David steps around me, shielding me with his body, "I believe my wife asked you a question. What are you doing here?"

He refuses to look at David, instead focusing on me, "You're pregnant? You lied to me!"

David takes a step toward him, "Do not speak to my wife like that!"

Landon laughs caustically, "Your wife? Oh, it's all 'my wife' now. Where were you when I was fucking her though? I'm pretty sure you couldn't have given two shits she was your wife then. No, you were too busy fu—"

David lands a solid punch into Landon's face and he stumbles into the bricks. I scream out in fright, backing further into the doorway.

David stands over him and growls, "Don't fucking curse in front of my son!"

Landon stands back up, wiping blood from his mouth, his eyes never leaving mine. "I guess I've been laboring under a false pretense here—thought you two were divorcing, that's obviously not the case. I just stopped by to say Happy Birthday, Elizabeth. Sorry to ruin your night." He turns and goes back to his Tahoe.

David looks at me, confusion etched over both of our faces. "Did he just leave...just like that? He didn't even try to swing back..."

I nod, while swallowing a lump in my throat. David closes the front door and locks it behind us. Tears prick my eyes and he wraps me up in a hug. "Come here, Birthday Girl. Let's not let an asshat like Landon Scott ruin our night. He knows I'm back permanently now—that should put an end to these surprise visits."

I nod against his chest, wanting to agree with him—more than anything. The problem is that I knew Landon better than he did and his eyes said that he wasn't finished.

CHAPTER THIRTY-FIVE
David

December 14, 2014

(28 weeks)

I place another log on the fireplace. "Thanks, David. I can't get warm."

I smirk over to where she's bundled up in three blankets on the couch. "And you're sure you want a bowl of ice cream right now, babe?"

She smiles and pats her stomach, "Well, someone's craving it. I'd rather have a salad, but this kid is demanding sweets!"

I chuckle and head for the freezer as she calls after me, "Do you really think we're going to get a blizzard over the next few days?"

I grab the ice cream and begin dishing it out, "Hard to say, babe. You know how hard it is to predict the weather around here. With all this hype, I wouldn't be surprised if it missed us completely."

She sighs, "It'd be nice to have a white Christmas for once."

I place the bowl of rocky road ice cream in her lap before joining her on the couch. "Beth, even if we got thirty-six inches of snow, I doubt there'd be any left on the ground by Christmas—"

—"*And we're back with our top story of the night, Blizzard Watch 2014. Ryan, what can you tell us?*"

"*Thanks, Lynn. Folks, this storm is no joke. Our early models show this storm strengthening as it moves into the area later tonight. As you can see, our viewing area is clear now, but we expect visibility to begin decreasing in the early morning hours. Travel is highly discouraged and remember if you have pets, tonight is not a night to leave them outside. We're expecting five to ten inches on the ground by mid-morning tomorrow, but snow will increase again around lunch-time. High winds will create white-out conditions and then we're expected to get an additional ten to twenty inches. Lynn, back to you."*

Beth gestures to me with a spoon full of ice cream, "I told you...storm of the century."

Her cell phone chirps and she glances down.

I mute the television, "Who is it?"

She sighs, "Lauren. She wants me to go up to the office and print out tomorrow's schedule, so we can call patients and reschedule if we get snowed in."

I stretch my feet toward the fire, "Why isn't she doing it?"

Beth looks up from the phone screen, "Oh, I forgot to tell you! Mike's mom came into town this weekend and they were having some big dinner thing. Lauren's been a nervous wreck."

"Betsy? Oh man, I hate that I'm missing her. She used to give me all kinds of shit back in the day—I don't think I've seen her in at least a year."

"Apparently, she's not a big fan of Lauren's, so it's probably best we're not over there."

I stand up, "Ah, she'll come around. Lauren grows on you—kind of like a fungus."

Beth swats my leg, "Rude."

I head to the door, "I'll go. You stay here."

She smirks up at me, "Yeah, if you knew what you were doing

that'd be awesome. Plus, you know Lauren would kill me if she knew you were going through patient records—she's already had people thrown in jail for violating patient privacy, I'd hate to see what she does to you."

She puts her now empty bowl of ice cream on the side table and stands up, pressing her hands into her lower back. "I'll run up there and be home in five."

"Are you sure? I can go with you."

She comes over and leans into me, "I'm a big girl, David. I got it. You should stay here and keep that fire going," she trails her hand down my arm lightly, giving me chills. "I might want to strip down and let you warm me up in front of it later."

I bite back a groan, "Okay, go, but hurry back." I tuck her hair behind her ear and take her mouth with mine.

Letting her walk out that door is a decision I'll regret for the rest of my life.

CHAPTER THIRTY-SIX
Beth

I finish printing the schedule I need and double check that the phone numbers are listed correctly on it. The sky looked ominous, but everything remained calm for the moment. It was hard to imagine that things could change so drastically in just a matter of hours.

As if he's feeling ignored, little man starts kicking up a storm. I giggle and place a hand on my belly, feeling his little body moving around. "Almost done, little guy. Then we'll go back home to Daddy."

I grab my purse, tucking my phone into the back pocket of my jeans. I shut off the lights and unlock the back door, pushing it open and into a man's body.

I try to jump back inside, but the door is wrenched from my hands.

Landon.

He stalks toward me in the unlit back hallway, "Thought you'd get away with it, didn't you?"

The blood is rushing in my ears and his voice sounds so far away, "G-g-get away w-w-with w-w-what?" *C'mon mouth, don't fail me now.*

He looks down at my belly and sneers, "You promised me that night that you hadn't slept with him, but you lied to me. You lied like the whore you really are!"

I start calculating the distance between him and the door. If I could slide around him, I could make it. I had to distract him though. "Landon, I don't know what you're talking about, I didn't lie to you."

He laughs and the sound fills me with dread, "Oh, I didn't realize I was dealing with the Virgin Mary here. Immaculate conception got ya down?"

He glances away and I take the only chance I'm going to get. I try to push my way around him and toward the door. The problem is that Landon's a whole foot taller and outweighs me by at least one hundred pounds. He throws his body into mine and I slam into the wall before falling back into his arms.

He takes a fistful of my hair and slams my head into the wall again. The blow stuns me and my head immediately feels fuzzy. He effortlessly turns me until my back is flush with the wall. His hand reaches out and strokes my face, "Look what you made me do, Elizabeth. I don't want to hurt you, but you can't pull shit like that again. Okay?" He speaks to me as if I'm a small child.

I spit into his face, "Fuck you, Landon. You think David is going to let you get away with this?"

His fist connects with my jaw and it pops loudly. I try to close my mouth and pain shoots up into my ear. *It's dislocated...or broken—probably both.*

I shakily bring my hand up and wipe away blood from the corner of my mouth. *Don't cry...do not cry.*

Landon pins me in with his arms on either side of my face, "Look around you, pretty girl. Do you see Davey anywhere in this fucking building?"

My body starts to tremble, but I refuse to shed a tear in front of him. I told David five minutes—it's probably been fifteen by now.

FORSAKING ALL OTHERS

"What? No tears for me? You once claimed to love me and now you don't even have the decency to feel ashamed of your actions."

David, please come looking for me. I plead the words over and over again in my head. I close my eyes, if I could just stall him—

Crack!

I gaze up at the ceiling, the room spinning around me. *How did I get down here?*

Landon snarls the words from somewhere above me, "Goddammit Elizabeth. You fucking answer me when I'm talking to you!"

I can smell the whiskey on him. It's as if it's seeping through his pores. The sickly sweet smell turns my stomach. I move my head away from him to retch onto the tile.

He yanks me up by my arm, "Stop making me hurt you. Be a good girl."

The sudden movement causes pain to radiate through my skull. He pushes the door open with one hand while the other keeps me in a firm grip. I'm seeing double right now—it's not like I can escape, no matter how badly I want to do just that.

I scan the parking lot, praying to see David's truck. Landon hits a button and the lift-gate goes up. He pushes my head down and I scream out in pain as my head connects with the vehicle floor.

He presses himself up against me and I can feel how hard he is. *He's getting off on this?*

The thought makes me want to vomit again.

He grabs a fistful of my hair and begins thrusting against me, "It's okay if you're feeling shy in front of me. I know it's been awhile since we were intimate. I bet I still know how to make you moan though."

What the hell is wrong with him?

The baby begins kicking in earnest now, startled by a stranger's voice. Hot tears spill down my cheeks and I try to push myself up. He makes a disapproving sound and yanks both arms back, forcing my head back onto the floor.

I jerk involuntarily at the feel of cold metal around my wrists. *No!*

I push my body back, trying to free myself. My body connects with his pelvis and I freeze.

"Greedy girl, you'll just have to wait a bit longer."

He roughly pulls me up and into the back of the Tahoe, closing the gate before I can move. I'm propped up between the back seat and the glass, blood is dripping from my mouth onto my belly and I fight back another wave of tears.

I have to stay strong and think of a way out.

CHAPTER
THIRTY-SEVEN
David

I look up at the clock. It's been twenty minutes—she should've been home by now. I grab my phone and dial her number.

It rings several times, *"Hey, you've reached Elizabeth Greene. You know what to do."*

I try to shrug off the feeling that something's wrong, but I can't. I stare at the fire before making up my mind. I'll just go up there and she'll get onto me for being overprotective.

Yeah.

She's fine.

I grab a coat and jump into my truck.

Once I reach the office though, the bad feeling increases. Her SUV is sitting dark in the parking lot.

I bang on the back door, praying that she throws it open. I'll take her being upset over the feeling currently residing in my gut.

I dial her phone again. It rings a few times and goes back to voicemail. Feeling frustrated, I dial Lauren.

"David? Thank God you called. I see where Mike gets his interrogation skills from. Betsy is driving me—lovely. I can't wait."

I can tell she's talking to someone else in the background, "Lauren—I'm gonna need you to get over to the office. Beth came up here to print out schedules like you asked, but she's not answering her phone now and I'm locked out of the building."

Lauren goes silent, "David, I didn't text her to go up there—" She covers the phone, but I can still faintly hear her, my heart is racing in my chest. If she didn't text her, then who did?

"Dave, Mike and I are on our way. Give us a couple of minutes."

I hang up, feeling completely helpless. I'm worried that she's lying inside that building hurt or worse, that someone followed her in. I'm considering breaking a window when Mike pulls up, lights flashing on his truck. They must've run every light to get here as quick as they do.

Lauren's hands shake as she unlocks the door and hits the light switch. The hallway illuminates my worst nightmare. Beth's purse is overturned, the contents scattered on the floor. Her coat and keys are together near what looks like vomit.

I'm shaking with fear and rage, while Mike has gone into full-blown detective mode. A small bloody hand print confirms my worst fear—someone took Beth and she fought like hell to stop him.

Mike grabs his cell phone and presses several buttons, "Shit! Laur—call 911—do not under any circumstances tell them I was here. David, get in the truck!"

Lauren is still standing with her hand over her mouth, in shock. "Mike, what's going on?"

He glances down at his phone again. "She somehow made it out of here with her phone on her," He holds it up to show us, "Whoever has her is outside the city, heading south."

He kisses her, "Just do what I said. Tell them you came up here to meet her and found this—don't touch anything."

She nods numbly and watches us go.

Mike starts the truck and reaches under the seat. He presses a

.40 caliber Smith & Wesson into my hand before securing his Glock. "We're gonna need these."

CHAPTER
THIRTY-EIGHT
Beth

My head bounces painfully against the back glass as we travel down a dirt road. Landon's been singing along to the radio as if he's on a leisurely drive in the country—maybe in his mind that's what this is.

"Elizabeth, do you know how long I had to watch you, just waiting for an opportunity like this? You really hid the fact that you let that bastard knock you up though. I mean, here I thought I'd show up on your birthday and you'd welcome me with open arms. Would anyone blame me? I've spent all this time searching for Katya—I deserved some happiness in my life. You had to fuck it up though—coming to the door with your swollen stomach. It messed up my fantasy."

I try to move my mouth to speak, but my jaw has swollen to the point it's frozen. My words come out sounding slurred, "What about Katya? Why are you giving up on her?"

Maybe if I reasoned with him, he'd realize what a mistake this was. My phone vibrates in my back pocket and I give a silent prayer of thanks that the ringer is off. I try to reach into it, my shoulder popping painfully in the process. I've almost got my hands around it when Landon answers me.

"Elizabeth, you're going to see Katya. She'll be so pleased to have some company."

He stops the SUV abruptly and my hands fall from my pocket.

FORSAKING ALL OTHERS

I scream silently.

He pops the lift-gate and lifts me up into his arms as though he's a groom carrying his bride over a threshold. I try to take in my surroundings with the light from his vehicle as guidance.

I'm in the middle of nowhere.

He carries me up the porch steps of an old farmhouse that probably should've been condemned decades ago.

"Honey, I'm home!" Landon laughs at his joke and continues on through the house, turning on lamps in the process. The house smells of dust and the lights illuminate mouse droppings covering nearly every surface.

He sets me down in the hallway and takes off my handcuffs, "Now, I'm only doing this because you're not going to run again. Right?"

I nod and rub my wrists gratefully. He hits a light switch in the hall and opens a door to reveal stairs going down. I back up a couple of steps and shake my head no.

He squeezes my arm, "Don't be a bitch. We have a houseguest who's been dying to meet you."

He follows me down the stairs, pushing me down each step. I stop at the foot of the stairs, not willing to move another inch. Landon ends up dragging me across the dirt floor. I begin screaming the minute I see her.

CHAPTER THIRTY-NINE
David

We're driving much faster than I would normally be comfortable with, bouncing up and down back country roads. All I can think of is getting to Beth though. Mike has me manning the app, tracking her cell phone.

The only time either one of us speaks is when he asks me for an update on her location and I give it. Otherwise, the truck is deathly quiet.

She's about twenty-five miles from our location. It looks like she stopped somewhere north of New Home. I silently urge the truck to go faster.

Beth

Beth

Beth

Every heartbeat pounds out her name.

I'm coming, baby.

Hold on.

I'm coming for you.

CHAPTER
FORTY
Beth

I thought she was dead. Then her eyes popped open and I began screaming again as she silently watched me.

I think back to the girl I saw in the photo at Landon's house, the girl whose face is plastered across billboards. The girl in front of me looks nothing like that.

Gone is the dark brown hair.

Her hair has been bleached until it's as blonde as mine.

She is severely emaciated and has bruises covering her once perfect skin.

She's wearing a replica of my wedding dress, but hers is filthy and ripped. I glance down and see blood between her thighs and I have to look away in horror.

"K-katya?" My voice shakes.

She nods slightly, never breaking eye contact with me.

Landon pulls me back to my feet, "Now, that we're all acquainted, let's get started. Did you see all the hard work I went to for you, Elizabeth? I tried to get her look just right, but no matter how hard I tried, she couldn't compare to you."

I try to focus on something else, the bile rising up in my stomach, but instead I see my wedding picture lying on a rusted metal table.

I point to it, "Is that my picture? You're the one who broke in and stole it that night!"

He bends my finger back until it snaps, and I scream in pain. "It's rude to point at people, Elizabeth! Davey let you get away with so much, but not me. I'm going to make you into a proper lady."

My finger is throbbing and I know without looking that he broke it. He pushes me back until I'm sitting in a chair before going over to the metal table and looking over something. "Are we ready? Good."

He holds up a small knife and I push myself out of my chair, "Nooo…" I stumble and fall onto my knees before I begin crawling toward the stairs. *I've got to get out of here. I've got to find help…for both of us.*

Landon grabs me by my hair and pushes me back into the chair, "Do I need to use the handcuffs again?"

I shake my head violently, causing more pain. Katya continues to stare blankly at me.

He runs the back of the knife down my cheek, "Good girl. See—you're learning. Now, I know you're probably as anxious as me to consummate this relationship, but there's one small problem—" He brings the knife down to my stomach and I stiffen immediately, "I can't let this go unpunished."

My blood is like ice in my veins. He gently traces designs against my stomach with the knife. I don't move a muscle. I can't let him hurt my baby. Katya's eyes widen with understanding and her lip begins to tremble.

I look away from her. I will not allow this monster to break me.

"Landon, what are you doing? You don't want to hurt me."

He smiles sweetly at me, "Of course I don't want to hurt you, sweet girl. I love you. I can't allow you to have any piece of him though. You belong to me. We're going to cut that reminder out and you'll be mine again. Just like before."

I feel the urge to pass out, but I can't lose consciousness. I fight to stay awake. I take a deep breath to steady myself, and place my hands on his arms, stroking gently. I resist the urge to vomit on him. "Landon, I've missed you. And I know that you're mad, but if you try to cut this baby out of me, I'll bleed to death. We're too far away for help to get here." I choke up and continue talking through the tears, "Please don't make me leave you when I just got back."

I don't mean a damn word of it, but I need him to think I do. He drops the knife into the dirt and pulls me into him. "I've waited six months to hear those words from you. Six long months." He kisses the top of my head before stepping back to look at me, "You're right. I can't take a risk like that with your life." I close my eyes in relief. Maybe if I'd kept them open, I'd have seen what was coming.

Katya screams out a warning just as Landon's fist connects with my abdomen. The blow knocks the air out of my lungs and I sink to the dirt floor, gasping for air. My stomach contracts painfully.

He stands over me, "You are mine, Elizabeth, and you will not walk out of here pregnant with that bastard's kid."

His foot comes up to kick me and I roll, my ribs taking the brunt of it. His fist comes down again and he connects with my belly before I can move. The pain is excruciating and I see spots, but I refuse to pass out. I will die fighting for my little boy.

Katya's screams pierce the air and I fight the urge to tell her to shut the fuck up as I dodge blows and kicks. I run my hand through the dirt and connect with the knife. I read the *Outlander* series a few years ago and I remember the clansmen teaching Claire how to fight with a knife. I clench it tight in my fist and try to remember how to effectively use it.

Landon grabs a fistful of my hair, dragging me up off the ground. "Stop fighting me. I don't want to hurt you. It'll all be over soon."

Just as he gets me up, I reach back and stab at him. I mistakenly hit a rib and pain jolts down my arm, almost causing me to drop it.

He glances a blow off the side of my head and the room spins, but I hold that knife like it's a lifeline. This time when I stab, the blade sinks in and Landon roars in pain, "You fucking bitch! You stabbed me!"

He lets go of my hair and I fall forward onto my hands and knees. I try to gather my bearings when he puts me in a headlock and hauls me back up, "I tried to make this easy for you, but now— I'm afraid to say—it's going to hurt you...a lot." He applies pressure on my throat, instantly cutting off my air supply.

My feet kick wildly in the air, black spots dancing in the corners of my eyes. I claw at his arms, his face—anything I can get within reach, but he just applies more pressure and I know this is it.

My eyes are streaming tears.

"Beth?"

I'm dying.

I can hear David's voice, but he sounds so far away.

David

I'm so sorry

I tried to save our baby

I tried to save us both, but I'm not strong enough

Landon roars in anger and loosens his grip enough for me to suck in a breath before he tightens it again.

"Oh my God—Beth!"

FORSAKING ALL OTHERS

I try to open my eyes, but everything goes dark.

CHAPTER FORTY-ONE
David

Mike parked and the minute we opened the truck doors, we could hear screaming. I didn't think twice, I just ran inside, yelling her name. It took us a minute to figure out that the screaming was coming from below us.

I bound down the basement stairs, gun drawn, and the sight is something that will forever be ingrained in my memory. I grew up hunting—Mike and I would even take weekend trips together every fall. I'm not one to miss my mark, but seeing my wife struggling in Landon's arms as he slowly chokes her—I've never felt so helpless. I'm afraid with as much as she's struggling, that I'll hit her by mistake. That's a risk I can't take right now. I'm so focused on getting a clear shot that I miss the woman in the corner. I don't notice her until she lunges at Landon, sinking something in between his shoulder blades. He drops Beth and turns on the woman.

I scoop Beth's limp body up in my arms and Mike takes the shot. I lay her back down in the dirt, ready to perform CPR, when she sucks in a ragged breath.

"David... are you really here?" Her voice is barely above a whisper.

I rock her in my arms and she cries out in pain, "I've got you, baby." I gently lay her back and see that she's drenched in sweat.

"Mike— we're going to need to call an ambulance. She's in

bad shape." I try to keep the emotion out of my voice, but her body is so battered.

She screams out in pain again, and I frantically search for what's hurting her.

"We're going to need an ambulance for both of them. We just found Katya Egorichev."

I grind my teeth together.

Mother fucker.

Beth screams and tries to clench my shirt before losing consciousness again.

Mike's face goes white and I follow his gaze to where blood is pooling between my wife's legs.

No no no!

I don't even see him whip out his phone, I'm so focused on stopping the bleeding.

"Beth, stay with me baby. Hold onto my voice. We're going to get you help."

Katya rocks back and forth, crying silently. "I tried to save her...I'm so sorry—I tried."

Mike wraps his jacket around her shoulders, while giving someone on the phone our GPS coordinates.

"How long will it take an ambulance to get to us?"

Beth begins panting and tries to sit up, forcing another gush of blood into the dirt.

"No, dammit, I don't have that kind of time. One of the female victims is twenty-eight weeks pregnant and in active labor due to trauma. How fast could you get a chopper in the air?"

I stare back at Beth's ashen face. She can't be in labor...it's too soon.

Mike roars into the phone, "Fuck! I'm aware that we're under a blizzard warning—I've got two women who need immediate medical attention!"

He paces back and forth as I cradle Beth in my arms. I try not to focus on what his actions mean for us, I refuse to let my wife and son die on the dirt floor of an abandoned farmhouse basement. I gently lift her in my arms and she moans.

"I got you, baby. We're going to get you help."

I nod at Mike as I lift her limp body in my arms, "Tell them I'll meet them, but I can't sit here and wait. She doesn't have that kind of time!"

Mike repeats my words and lifts Katya, the phone pressed to his ear the entire time. I carry Beth up the stairs, her blood soaking through her jeans and onto my hands.

Sweet Jesus.

I need more time with her.

If that mother fucker isn't dead yet, I'm going to be the one to personally send him straight to Hell.

CHAPTER
FORTY-TWO
Beth

I'm weighted down, like I'm sinking underwater.

Pain.

Everything hurts.

I thought death would be painless, but my body is in agony.

My abdomen feels like it's caught in a vice and the squeezing pressure takes my breath away.

I need to climb out of my body.

This is excruciating.

"Beth, baby—don't you dare leave me! Do you hear my voice? Hold onto it. Stay here!"

The disembodied voice breaks off in a sob… it sounds like David, but that can't be right.

The rocking movement jars my body and I want to cry, but no sound comes out.

Help me, David.

CHAPTER FORTY-THREE
David

Mike and I load both women into his truck. He gestures back toward the house—"Go, I'll catch up with you!" He tosses me his cell phone, "They'll get you to the chopper. Hurry—this storm won't hold back much longer."

I don't need another reminder—I navigate the dirt roads, every bump in the road causing sounds of anguish from both Katya and Beth.

The 911 operator remains calm, guiding me toward help. Beth is lying across the front seat with her head in my lap. Every little moan or sharp exhale is a reminder that she's still holding on, but for how much longer?

I glance up into the rearview mirror and see Katya staring blankly ahead, trembling every so often. I can't even begin to fathom what she went through for the last four months—if it's anything like what Beth went through in the last half hour, it's a damn miracle she's even alive.

I turn off the dirt road and back onto the highway when I see police roadblocks. I pull up just as the helicopter touches down onto the roadway and I feel myself choking up.

I throw the truck into park and gently slide Beth's head off my lap. One of the officers runs over, "Is the pregnant patient in the front or back seat?"

I numbly point at the front and he shouts over to the trauma team exiting the helicopter. Within moments, they have her on a stretcher and are getting vitals.

"BP is dropping!" One nurse calls out to another and I jog after the stretcher.

"Sir, you're going to have to follow us. There's not room."

"My wife—that's my wife and son."

The officer places his hand on my arm, "We'll escort you to the hospital. I understand we have another female victim though?"

I pinch the bridge of nose. Jesus—Katya. I open up the back door and the officer directs me to the seat next to her. "Can you ride back here with her? I'm going to get you to your wife as fast as possible."

I sit down next to Katya, unable to process what's going on around me.

I didn't tell her goodbye.

I just let them take her. What if that's the last time I see her—I can't let myself finish that thought.

Katya surprises the hell out of me when she reaches across the seat to take my hand in hers.

It doesn't matter how fast the cop up front is driving—I feel like I'm playing beat the clock.

Did I give them enough information?

What if they can't treat her without me there?

"We almost there?"

He nods, "I'll have you there in five minutes. Hang tight, man."

CHAPTER FORTY-FOUR

Beth

"Female, age thirty-one. Twenty-eight weeks pregnant... possible placental abruption. In route."

I drift off again. It hurts too much to stay awake. I'm being poked and prodded—*why won't they leave me alone?*

"Elizabeth, can you open your eyes and look at us?"

I try to force my eyes open, but they remain closed. I shake my head at the voice.

"ETA less than five minutes. We'll need a team prepped and ready to go. Patient has lost a lot of blood...signs of fetal distress."

Little man.

I'm so sorry, baby.

I failed you.

Another contraction hits me and I lose my breath. It eases up, only for another one to hit.

I can't catch my breath.

I feel the darkness pulling me under and I'm so tired of fighting it.

I'm just about to give in when I hear his voice as clearly as if he's sitting right next to me, *"Elizabeth Marie, don't you dare stop fighting! You keep breathing, in and out. One breath at a time. Keep fighting for my grandbaby in there. He needs his mama to be strong and brave. You hold on and when you pull through, tell that son of mine that I was always proud of him. Always, Elizabeth."*

John?

"Elizabeth? We're landing and we're going to get you help. Hold on!"

They pull me from the helicopter and into the frigid cold. I can hear voices all around me. It's as if the entire hospital is up here on the roof.

The voices that were just with me yell out information to the voices that are taking me.

I try to stay alert, but I fade out.

"Elizabeth, breathe in. This is all going to be over soon."

I don't have a choice.

The darkness takes over.

CHAPTER
FORTY-FIVE
Beth

I hear beeping and struggle to open my eyes. The lights damn near blind me so I immediately close them again.

"There you are! Here let me grab the lights." The lights dim and I open one eye slowly. When it doesn't cause piercing pain through my skull, I open the other one.

I look over at a nurse wearing a sympathetic smile. "You've been to Hell and back tonight, haven't you?"

I hear a soft hissing sound and realize I'm on oxygen—again. I try to open my mouth, but find that I can't. I ask through my teeth, "D-David?"

I wince from the pain it causes and the nurse comes closer, "Bless your heart. Your jaw was broken and it took the surgeon a little bit of time to get it realigned. Unfortunately, they had to wire your jaw shut so it will heal properly."

I nod and see my right index finger is splinted. The nurse follows my gaze, "Your finger was broken, along with three of your ribs. You most likely have a concussion as well."

I nod again, not knowing what to say. I place my hand on my belly and that's when I realize, I'm no longer pregnant.

My eyes fill with tears and I try to brush them away, but my entire face is bruised and the slightest touch sends a jolt of pain from my head down to my toes.

The nurse steps closer to me, "You had an abruption—your

placenta detached from your uterus during the trauma."

I think I've heard enough. I know she probably means well, but I can't handle this. The tears fall freely down my face and I let the darkness pull me back under again.

Chapter
Forty-Six
David

I rushed into the *Covenant* emergency room, desperate for information. When a nurse pulled me into a consult room and told me that Beth was undergoing an emergency C-section, I dropped to my knees in anguish.

I begged and pleaded to be taken to her, but was denied due to the severity of her injuries. When the nurse began listing the preliminary trauma that had been discovered, I came so fucking close to throwing a chair through the window.

They put me in a family waiting room, where Lauren joined me in pacing. Her face was splotchy from crying, "She's gotta be okay, David. She's so strong."

I bit my lower lip and looked down at the floor. I noticed my hands and clothes were stained red with her blood and that's what finally sent me over the edge.

I sank into a chair and wept. I cried for Beth and the pain she had to endure—pain I should've been able to keep her safe from. I also cried for my little boy. He must've been so scared.

I bowed my head and prayed.

I prayed that he didn't suffer and then I bargained for my wife's life.

FORSAKING ALL OTHERS

"Mr. Greene?" A nurse walks over to me.

I stand back up, "Is she okay? Can I see her?"

She places a hand on my arm, "She came through the surgery like a champ. She's in recovery right now, but as soon as I can—I'll take you up to her room."

I breathe a sigh of relief.

"And Mr. Greene?"

My eyes meet hers. "Yes?"

"Congratulations—you've got a son. He was born right after midnight. He weighs two pounds, eight ounces—but he's a fighter. They've transferred him to the NICU. As soon as I have more information for you—I'll be back."

I raise my face to the ceiling, "Thank you."

My family is safe.

CHAPTER
FORTY-SEVEN
Beth

I open my eyes and the sky is a light shade of grey. I'm still on oxygen and back in a room similar to the one I woke up in after the car accident.

I have this horrible fear that the doctor is going to come in and tell me that it was all a dream—David and our baby. Tears prick my eyes and I let them spill over.

What if it all was just a dream?

I'm in an empty hospital room. I glance down at my body through the top of the hospital gown.

My ribs are an explosion of black and purple bruises, proof that I lived through a nightmare. I gently push the blankets down and lift up my gown. My tummy is slightly rounded still, but soft to the touch. There's a fresh horizontal scar and my eyes well up with tears again.

They had to cut him out of me.

I lower the gown and pull the covers back up, focusing on grey skies and falling snow beyond the window.

CHAPTER FORTY-EIGHT
David

I try to get comfortable in the hospital chair. My entire body aches, but I refuse to leave her side. I pulled myself together long enough for the nurse to get me into the room with Beth.

Once I saw her, I fell apart again. Her face is so swollen, she's almost unrecognizable. The doctor said her jaw was broken in two places and that he had to wire it shut so it has time to heal. She suffered a concussion, broken ribs, scalp lacerations, and a broken finger as well.

He pulled me outside the room and told me that she most likely suffered blunt force trauma to the abdomen and that led to placental abruption—where the placenta is torn away from the uterus. Landon could have killed them both.

Had we not gotten there when we did...they both would've died.

Beth lost a lot of blood, but by some miracle, doesn't need a transfusion.

"David?"

I jump up from the chair and rush over to her, "I'm here, baby." She begins weeping and I take her gently into my arms, "Shhhh...I've got you. You're safe."

Her hand shakily comes up to my face, "David, I'm sorry. I tried—I tried to fight for him." Her voice breaks again and I realize that no one's told her.

SHANNON MYERS

I turn her carefully so that she's facing me, "Beth—baby, you did so good. You protected our little guy."

"What do you mean?" I know he's trying to soften the blow, but there's no way to make this better. They took a piece of my heart when they cut my son from my womb.

He strokes the back of my hand gently, "He's alive, baby. Our son made it."

My chin quivers and I start crying again, "He's okay?—but it's too soon. We never even came up with a name."

David looks away from me and focuses on the swirling snow, his voice is almost a whisper. "He has a name...Kaden John Greene."

"Kaden? How did you come up with that?" I hope he can still clearly understand me as I'm talking through my teeth.

He looks back at me, "It means, 'fighter.' When they told me he made it, I knew he was going to need a name that was as strong as he was. Is it okay?"

I nod, too overcome to immediately speak.

I take a deep breath, my ribs protesting angrily. I push through the pain. "I heard him."

David looks at me, confused. "Kaden? You heard him?"

I shake my head, "I heard your dad's voice. In the helicopter. I wanted to give up—I was exhausted and my entire body hurt. I was ready to quit fighting when I heard him. He told me to be brave for his grandbaby. So, I fought until the nurses took over."

David lowers his head against mine, his eyes bright with unshed tears, "He always had a knack for showing up when things were falling apart—I'm glad to know that dying couldn't stop him from looking out for you and Kaden."

I swallow hard, "He said something else too."

David's eyes hold mine.

I continue, "He said to tell you that he was always proud of you, David."

He covers his eyes with his hands and sobs before wrapping me up in his arms.

CHAPTER FIFTY
David

4 Days Later...

It turns out Beth was right. We lived through the "storm of the century." The snow started falling almost immediately after we arrived at the hospital and it didn't let up for over twenty-four hours.

We've spent almost every waking minute in the NICU with our baby boy. They took him there right after delivery and intubated him.

We were both emotional wrecks when we stepped foot into the NICU that first time. Beth got out of her wheelchair and stepped up to the incubator. "Hey Kaden, it's your mama. I love—" Her voice cut off and I looked over to see she was weeping silently. I wrapped my arms around her and joined in. His tiny little body was glowing blue under the bili lights—something that was supposed to help prevent jaundice. It was fucking painful seeing the various tubes and wires running out of his little body, knowing he should still be in Beth's tummy.

Once they were sure he was out of the woods, one of the nurses showed us how to do what's called kangaroo care with Kaden. I volunteered to go first and I'll admit, I was a nervous wreck that first time. It was just me and him, skin to skin, with the ventilator and wires surrounding us. I was so scared to move, afraid I was going to jar something loose. He was so incredibly small in my arms and I was worried sick that I could break him.

Beth and I have settled into a routine of waking up and going to see him around eight every morning. Around noon, I'll beg her to go eat something and like clockwork every day, she refuses. She just wants to hold him, she wants him to know that she's here for him. I would argue with her logic, but just this morning, he reached his little hand up and grabbed onto her finger. It was all the confirmation she needed.

So, we stay with our baby until the sun goes down and from six to eight every night we sit in comfortable silence together, eating. Then, we'll go back to the NICU and stay until the wee hours of the morning. I'm exhausted, but I like knowing that they're both safe. And I'd gladly give up sleep for the rest of my life to ensure they're both okay.

It hurts her to talk. When she saw herself in the mirror that first time out of bed, I was worried sick that she'd fall apart. She touched the black and violet bruises on her face and neck, tears falling silently onto her cheeks.

I look over to where Lauren is sitting on the hospital bed, talking Beth's ear off. She catches my eye and gives me a small smile—and I feel like I just won the fucking lottery.

Her smile fades and she stares at the television. They've filled the screen with Landon's picture

"We're back tonight with the latest on the search for Landon Scott, the man involved in the disappearance of Katya Egorichev and the kidnapping of Elizabeth Greene. Egorichev was found severely dehydrated and suffering from malnutrition. She is being treated at a local hospital tonight. Elizabeth Greene was twenty-eight weeks pregnant when she was taken—she was severely beaten and had to undergo an emergency cesarean section. Both mom and

baby are recovering in the hospital tonight as well. Landon Scott was injured in an altercation with a police officer, but managed to flee the scene. His vehicle was found yesterday morning buried in a snow drift and blood inside the vehicle matched that found on scene. If you have any information on his whereabouts, you are urged to call Crimestoppers immediately..."

At least they left out the part about Katya having been beaten and raped daily since she went missing. I think the poor woman went through enough without the world knowing that. She told Mike when he went to visit her that she wanted to see Beth as soon as she was well enough. They share an unbreakable bond now.

"David? A little help please..."

I snap out of my thoughts to see Beth about to go into a full-blown panic attack while Lauren holds her arms.

Her chest heaves with each breath and I know that's gotta be hell on her ribs. I jump up and go to her.

"Beth—deep breaths, baby. He can't hurt you anymore."

She takes another shallow breath and whispers, "He's going to come back for me and Kaden—he's going to hurt him. I can't let him do that. David, you have to go warn the doctors and nurses."

She never once asked what happened to him and I hoped to never have to tell her.

"Beth, look at me." She turns with wide eyes. "He can't hurt you anymore. He will never hurt you again."

Lauren sucks in a breath and looks at me questioningly, "David?"

I shake my head, "He'll never be found."

Beth makes a small squeak of surprise, "You did something didn't you?"

I stroke her hair gently, never taking my eyes off of hers, "I took care of my family. That's all you need to know, baby."

I expect her to argue, but she surprises me when she whispers, "Thank you."

That's it. She doesn't ask me anything else—she just trusts me. I don't know if she even remembers me leaving her right after Kaden was born. I waited until I knew they were going to pull through and then met Mike. He took me back to my truck, which was still sitting at Beth's office and slipped me a piece of paper with the coordinates I needed.

Before I left, he grabbed me in a rough hug, "You call me once it's done and we'll take care of it together."

I simply nodded and left.

CHAPTER
FIFTY-ONE
David

I walked into yet another old farmhouse a few hours outside of town. The snow had finally stopped falling and as if it was a sign, the roads I needed were all clear.

Landon sat strapped to a chair in the middle of what was once a living room. I could see the blood stains on his shirt, where Beth and Katya managed to stab him. There was also a gunshot wound to his lower left leg. The bone jutted from the skin at an odd angle and blood had coagulated to the point that it looked almost like jelly. Mike never meant to kill him, reserving that right for me. His shot effectively maimed Landon to the point that he was no longer a threat.

His head was hanging down, but the minute he heard my footsteps that head shot up. He grinned when he saw it was me, Beth's claw marks had left bright red gashes down his face and arms.

He spit out blood, I'd have to thank Mike for that later. "Well, well...look who we have here. Davey."

Landon's words are mocking, even though he's the one bound to a chair. He nearly took everything from me—my entire world. He sat there with a smug look on his face, not realizing he wasn't going to be leaving here alive. I grabbed my phone and cranked up Linkin Park.

I quietly got what I needed, walking from room to room as I

did so, and he yelled after me, "What's the matter? You pissed because I got rid of the kid? You should be thanking me, asshole! Now, there's nothing tying you to her."

I ground my teeth together, but refused to say a word. Not that it mattered, he didn't wait for a response.

"Elizabeth shouldn't have fought me. I was doing her a favor—but the bitch didn't see it that way. You know, you were supposed to leave. She was mine—always mine."

His voice changed as he got lost in thought and I bided my time in another room. I had to keep my anger under control. I turned the hammer over and over again in my hand, focusing on the music.

"You know, I never wanted to hurt her—but I'm gonna be honest with you, Davey. The feel of her delicate little throat underneath my arm that night, squeezing and feeling her fight against me—it was invigorating. I'm getting hard just thinking about it—God, listen to me, chattering away. What about you, Davey? Ever wanted to see fear in her eyes?—Cause I gotta tell ya, you are not doing her any favors. You let her get away with everything. Women need boundaries—I taught her a few the other night, you can thank me for that later—"

I didn't let him finish this time. I calmly walked back in, swinging the hammer. I'd used it on countless jobs and never once considered what a perfect weapon it would make. The head of it connected with his right kneecap and the sound of his screams filled the room. I moved to the left one and poured all of my rage into the swing.

"C'mon man—" His voice had lost the confidence from a few moments ago and I smiled before putting him into a headlock. I didn't stop smiling as he began struggling in my arms, needing air.

I waited until he began going limp before I released him. He sucked in ragged breaths and I knelt down beside him.

"You're right, Landon. That was fucking invigorating!"

I drew back and swung the hammer into his ribs this time. Beth had three broken ribs on the right side, so I felt the need to inflict those same injuries onto him. He began coughing and his breaths turned shallow. *I may have collapsed his lung with that last swing.*

He looked up at me and his eyes held fear. I swore six months ago that I'd put him in the ground if he laid a finger on her.

I got right up in his face, "Not that I should waste my breath telling you this, but my wife and son are both alive—and they're going to stay that way. You wanna know why? Because only one of us is walking out that door today."

His eyes widened with understanding and I took sick pleasure in the fact that he was in no condition to reply.

I watched him struggle for each breath for a few more minutes. Then, I calmly retrieved my gun from the other room and emptied it into his chest. His glassy eyes stared at nothing as I reached for my phone, blood pooling under the wooden chair. I felt nothing.

"Mike, it's done."

EPILOGUE
David

18 Months Later…

I stare up at a cloudless sky, trees lining my view. I'm standing in the middle of a pecan orchard surrounded by the people closest to me.

What do you do when you almost lose the love of your life? If you're me, you marry her all over again.

Kaden spent the first four months of his life in the hospital. Everything was chaotic, with the majority of our time spent at the hospital. Beth was still recuperating from her injuries and the subsequent C-section. Once we got him home, it was like starting over. We had to figure out parenting without the nurses there to guide us. My beautiful wife was a natural though and she gave me confidence in my parenting abilities.

It took about a year to get into a good routine, but once I knew Kaden was healthy enough, I dropped to one knee and asked her to be mine all over again. I asked her to marry me, fully knowing both the good and the bad, and she said yes. Well actually, she laughed and said something along the lines of thinking that we already were, but she did agree to renew our vows.

Here I stand, under a small wooden arbor and pecan trees for miles. I look over at Mike and smile. He returns it, but his doesn't quite meet his eyes. He and Lauren broke up not long after Beth had Kaden. He won't talk about it, but I know he's still in love with her. This will be the first time he's seen her since, so I slap him on the shoulder and pull him in for a side hug.

Beth

My mother places flowers in my hair while Lauren finishes my makeup. Yes, my mother. I don't know if she had a change of heart or if my dad pushed her into it, but she showed up as soon as she knew I was in the hospital. She fussed over me and Kaden, never once saying "I told you so."

Louisa looks at her watch, "You're up, kid. You nervous?"

I smile, trying not to cry so I don't mess up all of Lauren's good work. "I'm not...just excited."

Lauren grumbles, "I'm a little nervous, to be honest. Lou—you got anything in that mom purse of yours to take the edge off?"

My mom shocks us all when she pulls a flask from her handbag and passes it to Lauren. "What?" she scoffs. "So, I drink. How else do you think I've gotten through all these years of quilting club at the church?"

We dissolve into laughter and I squeeze Lauren's hand.

David

The pastor walks up and greets us, spending an extra few minutes playing with Kaden. I've got him on my hip so Beth can get ready in peace. He's just started crawling and has yet to say a word that's intelligible, but his pediatrician assured us that it's completely normal in preemies. He loses interest in what the pastor is saying and begins shredding the rose on my lapel. I kiss his little hands and move him away.

Both of our moms come down the aisle to take little man off my hands. The music starts and I laugh. I begged Beth to play some country when she walked down the aisle, but she's chosen a Coldplay song instead. I would protest, but the lyrics are so damn perfect that I find myself fighting back tears. I would still call every second spent with her magic.

Lauren comes walking out and I see Mike's mouth drop open. He sucks air between his teeth and I grin. I glance up just as Beth comes walking down the aisle with her dad. She's only taken a few steps when someone on the back row stands up and walks over to her.

She sees the panic in my eyes and winks. One of her cousins begins snapping along to the music and someone else joins them. My aunt jumps up out of her seat and moves perfectly to the beat of the music.

Lauren skips back to where Beth is and they link arms. Two of her co-workers get up and join, along with several of my construction guys. They've obviously rehearsed the entire thing and kept it a secret.

A flash mob.

Only my wife. My *Glee*-loving wife.

Beth

My heart is pounding out a steady stomp-clap beat similar to the one in the song. Chris Martin's voice fills the orchard and one by one our wedding guests get up and join me in walking to David.

Seeing those big burly construction guys moving in perfect time makes me grin. David laughs in surprise and then I see the tears on his face. Everyone is snapping and moving in sync and the emotions overtake me.

I don't want anyone else, but you.

My mom has Kaden in her arms and my sweet baby boy gives me the sweetest smile, his eyes wide with excitement.

"Mama!" I look at Kaden in surprise and then up at David. He roughly rubs the back of his hand across his eyes, trying to stop the tears. *His first word.*

Chris Martin starts singing in a falsetto and several women join in singing as we make our way closer. Katya is sitting a few rows from the front and she gives me a bright smile. She came back to Texas from Colorado just for this. Her long brown hair is back and she looks so at peace. I give her a small wave.

Mike's eyes are laser-focused on Lauren and I squeeze her tighter. I don't know what happened between the two of them, but I have a feeling they'll find their way back to one another.

This is absolutely perfect. People begin splitting off and making their way back to their seats as we approach my groom. I'm within just a couple of feet when I trip over my own and fall right into him—his arms locking protectively around me.

I knew Beth was going to fall at some point. It's just who she is. I set her upright to a chorus of cheers and the pastor begins. I recite my vows, but my eyes communicate even more to her. I let her know that I'll always be the one to catch her when she falls. I'll hold her when the nightmares from that night show up. I'll never again let her think she's not the most important thing in my life.

Beth

For better. For worse.

That's the funny thing. We've had both.

I'd still choose him every time.

It might not be your typical fairy tale, but it's mine.

It's real. It's raw—it's the most beautiful kind of love. The kind that can come back from infidelity. The kind of love that can withstand the emotional and physical trauma of the last eighteen months. The kind of love that will fight and even kill if necessary. We aren't promised a 'happily ever after,' but I will keep choosing him—everyday. Isn't that the point of all of this? To find the person for whom your soul whispers, "This is the one."

And while it may not always be happy, we will live for each other forever after.

And that's enough for me.

The end.

SHANNON MYERS

ABOUT THE AUTHOR

Shannon lives in Lubbock, Texas with her husband, two sons, and the family dog Elvis. She is a sucker for a good romantic story and has a tendency to develop crushes on fictional characters. When she is not writing, she enjoys cooking, reading, and weekend DIY projects around the house.

Find her online at: http://shannonshaemyers.com